Stop Speaking Mexican!

The Price of an Education

Gloria Elena López

CONTENTS

DEDICATIONS

I dedicate this book to my parents, *Epifanio Reynaldo Trujillo y Maria Dolores Trujillo* who gave me the gift of languages by modeling a respect for English and Spanish at home from birth. My life has been enriched by the vast knowledge I have acquired speaking, reading, writing and listening in two languages.

Gracias a mis queridos padres.

I dedicate this book to my husband and my sons whose unconditional love has been a constant in my journey and recovery.

Gracias a mi querida familia.

I dedicate this book to anyone who has unresolved trauma from school based violence and has lived in silence with the long term effects of those memories. I wrote this book so you know the difference effective mental health counseling can make in your recovery process with PTSD.

No tienen que estar solos con sus memorias.

You do not need to be alone with your memories.

INTRODUCTION

There is no greater agony than bearing an untold story inside you.
Maya Angelou

***

I have lived my life haunted by the child abuse experienced during the school year 1962-1963 in a Colorado elementary school. All these years, I have wanted to rescue and advocate for the little girl who was trapped, tortured, shamed and forced to comply with the racist practices of a licensed teacher. In order to prepare myself for the hard work of talking about what happened to me at school all those years ago, I have had to unravel myself emotionally from age six through effective mental health therapy, specifically EMDR Eye Movement Desensitize and Reprocess Therapy.

I had learned to live with PTSD- Post Traumatic Stress Disorder; the guilt, anxiety, rage, torture, shame and denial associated with childhood abuse most of my adult life. I learned to mask my symptoms and pain in unhealthy ways throughout my adult life.

Today I know I was kidnapped from my classroom against my will and taken to my teacher's house as her private Mexican servant from September to May of that school year. She practiced this crime in broad daylight during the lunch hour when there were many potential witnesses. I was never the same child my parents entrusted to this licensed educator in September 1962. That year I learned and lived what it means to be second class in the United States of America. At my young age I knew it was the sound of my Spanish voice and the color of my skin that entitled her to treat me as she did. I was not her student; I was her personal property for nine months. She claimed three of the students assigned her as Mexican servants that school year, I was one of them. She took the liberty of imposing her racist beliefs and low expectations on myself and two other classmates for the next nine months in the privacy of her home. The effects of her criminal behavior disrupted my child development and derailed my career as a public-school educator. The Second class treatment I experienced as a Spanish speaker in first grade would resurface in my career as a bilingual teacher, graduate student and elementary principal.

I would love to say that first grade was amazing and my teacher was loving and accepting, but I would be lying to you and myself. I would love to say that her teachings did not shape me or influence my perception of myself as a human being, but I would be lying to you and myself. What happened in first grade was life changing! At age six I knew that the teacher's behavior was evil and hateful. Evidence of my integrity and brilliance came on the last day of school in May 1963 when I attempted to burn the materials I brought home from school using wood matches from our kitchen. I wanted to be rid of anything that would remind me of my teacher and her cruelty. I wanted to burn the memories of her abuse that continued until the last day of school. My attempts at closure on the last day of school were disrupted when family members put out the fire and never asked my reasons for burning the graded papers, leftover school supplies and a math workbook. On the last day of school I was attempting closure for the abuse experienced at age six and I was denied. I will carry this burden of trauma through my career, my marriage and raising my family.

In order to heal and close this painful chapter of my life, I had to end the internal conflict between the educated female who was hell bent on completing her professional career at all costs. This determined educated female who had studied the pedagogy and foundations of education and the school laws governing schools, now found herself confused about the laws and procedures governing schools. This professional educator was now in constant conflict with what she had learned in her professional development in public education. My child persona on the other hand demanded validation and justice for the unresolved trauma during the school year 1962. The long term effects of childhood abuse by a school official affected me, my entire public school career as a student, teacher, principal and colleague.

As an elementary teacher on recess duty I would witness many important life lessons on the playground between students. When one student would come to me crying and declare, "He pushed me down on purpose and didn't say sorry!" The other student would tell me, "Uh Uh, it was an accident." The student who fell down knew otherwise, he knew the behavior of the other student was on purpose and no accident because he didn't apologize. The outcome of such a process on a playground is that the other student apologized for their behavior to the one who landed on the ground then spent the rest of the recess standing against the wall in self reflection. This conflict was solved with two non-violent words, "I'm sorry".

At the age of six one does know when the actions of another are on purpose or an accident. At age six, I remember my teacher never apologized for her non teaching behavior, instead she normalized it with her daily routines.

A SPECIAL NOTE FROM THE AUTHOR

Before reading my book I need you to understand that the most important element of my recovery as a PTSD sufferer has been to reclaim my voice as the child who was abused at age six in an elementary classroom.. By empowering and healing my childhood voice, I am able to tell my story in its purest form.

This book is possible because I have recovered and contended with the painful school memories which were the source of trauma for most of my life. I have healed my inner child through EMDR and the weekly mental health therapy sessions with an effective and loving therapist. The anxiety, depression and low self esteem associated with PTSD has lifted and allowed me to heal emotionally and physically. My autobiography gives a voice to the six-year-old student who kept a painful secret for 62 years. This is for *Gloria Elena, the* first-grade student whose attempts to close this painful chapter were denied on the last day of school in 1962. Today, she is ready to talk about her educational journey from age six to retirement. America will hear, see and feel the long-term effects of racism on my psyche and career as a public school educator.

"A mi no me pueden tapar el sol con un dedo"
- Maria Dolores Trujillo, mi mama

Figuratively speaking: "You can not hide the obvious from me."

What is PTSD?

Through my own research on Post-Traumatic Stress Disorder (PTSD), I found it commonly defined as a disorder resulting from psychological and/or physical injuries. Some of the first diagnosed PTSD victims in this country were soldiers who returned from war traumatized by their experiences in the workplace while in the military. The "stress" demonstrated by these individuals in trying to return to domestic life defined how post trauma affected their lives. Their symptoms gave rise to terms such as flashbacks, triggers, intrusive thoughts, and emotional detachment which are common with PTSD. These words define what happens to a person who has been traumatized when their past memories take over their present state of mind. Triggers are usually sensory alerts which awaken the trauma because they are related in ways only the sufferer knows. Through my own education I have learned traumatic events can be physical and/or emotional in nature. A natural disaster, a car accident, the death of a spouse, parent or child or any near-death incident can become the source of trauma and result in a diagnosis of PTSD.

Intentional traumas are often the result of domestic violence and physical rape. These events occur because a person abuses their power over another human being. Through my own therapy and personal accounts, I would learn that School Based violence like kidnapping, child abuse and sexual harassment in schools are types of intentional traumas which occurred in my educational journey. These types of traumas are defined by the shame and fear experienced by victims who dare speak out. Sometimes these trauma symptoms can be delayed by suppression of memory until the day the victim comes to terms with total recall.

CHAPTER 1:
ELENA'S DREAM

The little girl who burned her books on the last day of first grade, grew up to be an elementary bilingual educator. I would become the teacher I needed in first grade and thereafter, an educator who respected, accepted, and embraced the linguistic differences of my students. My favorite childhood activity when I was alone was playing school of course. It was not only my favorite childhood play, but it was also my career goal. I remember walking among the tall *"girasol"*- sunflowers in the field close to our house all by myself. It was my favorite detour to get to the family garden by the river where I would meet my mom who was waiting for me at the river's edge with small watering buckets made for little people like me. I would help mom water the thirsty plants who needed more water than we could possibly haul. My mother would walk to the river by herself which were a few moments of silence just for her.

In the meanwhile, I would sit down under the tallest sunflowerI I could find and close my eyes. I would let *"markitas"*-ladybugs land on my arms and I would count them before they flew away. If I closed my eyes long enough and my mind was quiet, I could imagine myself growing up with a career. In this dream state I could see myself in a classroom with students teaching and helping them with their studies. I loved my dream of being a teacher and believed it could come true! My parents believed in my dream when they asked what I wanted to be when I grew up. I would reply, "I want to be a teacher." They knew the path to my dreams was going to school and getting good grades, so they instilled in me an expectation for academic success.

By the age of six, I was speaking, reading and writing in two languages, of that I am sure. Mom would help me write down spelling words for my classroom. She also wrote down math problems for me to practice and use in my lessons in the barn. This was of course my math practice which she checked later. I would take my sister's doll, Georgia, my stuffed chimpanzee -*Chango* and two other dolls handed down from my *prima* Debbie and go set up school in the *corral*. I would roll bales of loose bales of hay to create desks for students and a desk for me, the teacher. I also had the company of mice living among the bales of hay who now scampered among the bales as I moved them. I had to be careful not to step into the hubcap full of cow's milk left for the bull snake hidden between the bales of hay, which kept the mice population down.

I had pencils, paper and crayons for my students because mom saved all the extra school pencils just for me to play school! I even had a small broken chalkboard and a few broken pieces of chalk. I would copy the spelling words onto the chalkboard one at a time and say the letters out loud. My students of course repeated the letters and read the words I had written on the chalkboard in their tablets. I would erase the spelling words and write a math problem on the board. I would instruct my students to write down the math problems on their paper and we would answer together. I knew how to copy the numbers mom had written down from a piece of Chief tablet. I knew how to represent number values with slash marks and could demonstrate numbers added and subtracted to my imaginary students. I was always surprised when mom showed up. I could hear her singing or chanting my name," You who *Elena donde estas"*-Elena where are you?", as she made her way to the *corral* where she knew I loved to play school. I played school most days in the afternoon until mom came to check on me and help me take my dolls back to the house.

While I waited for the day when I could go to school with my brothers and sister, I was busy at home with *Mama*, I also called her mom. *Mama* and I had been together most days because I was the baby of the family and I had stayed home four years with her before I started school. My sister was four years older than I and my brothers older than she so I got to have *mama* all to myself while they were in school!

My *mama* worked hard all day and I spent a lot of time watching, learning and helping with household chores. We did not have electricity or running water at our house across the river so a job like washing clothes took all day long. I would help her fill the *"cajetes"*- metal tubs with cold water as soon as my two older brothers and sister left for school. Our water was stored in several metal barrels out on the shaded part of our porch. The water had been hauled from the *San Juan* which was a walking distance from our house. We hauled the water from the river on a large wooden sled pulled by a tractor or horses. I loved to ride the wooden sled to the river but I wasn't much help filling the barrels. That was a job my father and brothers had for our family two or three times a month. I just remember going along for the ride and seeing the amount of water lost from the barrels because the road was rough and rocky.

On laundry day, it was fun to stand on a stool and scoop up water in a can and pour it into mom's larger pail! My job was to fill mom's pail then I would try to guess how many cans it would take to fill up her large pail and count the number of cans it took to fill the larger bucket, a math lesson in probability. *Mama* corrected me if I messed up counting, so I learned to count accurately. *Mama* would warm up the water in large dish pans on top of the wood stove. She would send me to bring her wood for the stove to keep warming the water. I could bring a piece in each arm but that was enough. I would make several trips to the woodpile to keep the fire burning two pieces of wood at a time. I learned to count by twos by hauling wood for *mama* on wash day.

I would sort the clothes by colors for mom while she washed each item on a "*lavadero*"- a washboard. I knew all my colors in English and Spanish because she would test me as I moved clothes to the pile close to her. She would tell me, "*Me pones toda la ropa blanca aquí, las sábanas, las camisetas de los hombres y las medias*". I would put all the white clothes, the bed sheets, men's undershirts and socks in one pile. "I came to know the word *medias y calcetines* as two ways to say socks in Spanish. I would then sort all the clothes with colors like shirts, blouses, shorts and dresses into one large pile. The only clothes left then were the *lonas*-the blue jeans. By this time the water was brown from washing all the other clothes and mom would change the water for hot water she had been heating on the stove. She simply tipped over the *cajete* - a metal tub and emptied it on the spot, it was too heavy for us to manage together. Mom then emptied the hot water from the dish pans into a pail and began filling the cajete once again. She would then add several pairs of blue jeans into the hot water and then take a stick she used specially for this job and begin to poke the stick repeatedly into the jeans as they soaked in the water. This action made the water turn brown as the dirt came out of the blue jeans.

In my house, we spoke English and Spanish all the time. I don't remember a time in my life when I did not speak both languages. I didn't learn one before the other, instead I learned two languages at the same time. I was born bilingual from my mother's womb. I always remember my parents speaking both languages except Grandpa *Manuel* and Grandma *Teresita*, they spoke only in Spanish. I remember Grandma getting frustrated with her English speaking grandchildren who smirked when she attempted to speak English. She wanted to speak English so badly, it was a valuable language to my grandmother and she was happy her grandchildren spoke the language. My daddy spoke more English at home than mom, he had been a soldier in the WWll.

When we went to church, I got to read in Spanish and English, mom would track the lines for me and I would follow along. I could read the prayers I had learned to recite like, *"El Padre Nuestro "*- "The Lord's Prayer' '. I loved singing in church and learned the words to songs quickly. *El Padre*- the priest was Spanish and he loved to sing , *"Oh Maria, Madre Mía ", "Bendito, Bendito" and "Adios Reina del Cielo "*. I learned these songs just by listening and following the adults when they sang. It was even more fun to recognize the words on paper as I read them. I understood then that reading was talking on paper.

During the day, I didn't see daddy very much but mama would tell me, *"tu daddy anda en el rancho "* when I asked for him. He would leave early in the morning and go to Grandpa and Grandma's ranch across the river and he didn't come back until it was getting dark. He and grandpa *Manuel* had a lot of sheep and other animals and that meant daddy was busy all the time.

I loved the days we counted the sheep and lambs. I had helped feed the *"pencos"*, orphans whose mamas died right after they were born. Now that I was bigger, I got to help with the sheep count. Daddy made it a math lesson just for me! I could add and subtract numbers conceptually after working on the sheep ranch our *familia* owned. I learned by doing and watching others perform the tasks I would be expected to do later. My way of learning was not questioned nor was I punished because I watched others learn. I was expected to learn by doing. Daddy would tell me, "pay attention and watch".

I missed the company of my brothers and sister when they were at school, though they were four or more years older than me. I knew they would be home soon once mom started cooking again, she always had food ready for them when they got home. They were always hungry after the hour long school bus ride home, then they had to cross the San Juan river on a log bridge daddy made, then cross a field to get home. I could see the road on the other side of the river and the dust the school bus made as it made its way from one stop to another. I knew my brothers and sister had to climb down a steep hill to get to the river, then cross on the log bridge daddy made for our family. It was dangerous to cross, because the water ran over the log sometimes!

I would watch them race home once they crossed the river, they were all fast runners and seemed to get to the house quick! They immediately dropped their books and climbed into the kitchen chairs and began serving the delicious food mom prepared. Today *mama* prepared *papas con carne, homemade tortillas* and *chile colorado con huevo.* Mom had prepared potatoes with fried meat, fresh tortillas and red chili sauce with scrambled eggs. I sat and listened to them talk about their school day. My brothers and sister talked about their friends and teachers by name. They had funny stories to tell everyday. Soon I would have stories to tell at the end of my school day, I hoped they would be funny like their stories.

I wasn't afraid of going to school and being away from my parents. I knew that at the end of every day, the school bus would bring me home safely as it did my siblings. I knew that my brothers and sister's classrooms were on the second floor of the school and they would know to come get me at the end of the school day. I knew that I was ready to learn alongside other kids my age.

Daddy had taken me with him to register for first grade. I remember the secretary, Mrs. Kingsley had a lot of questions for daddy and he was quick to answer. Daddy spoke English very well and did not struggle understanding Mrs. Kingsley. The secretary told my dad that I would need to register under my legal name, *Gloria Trujillo* and not my middle name, Elaine or the Spanish version *Elena*. She informed dad that this was best for me because I had to get used to my legal name. Daddy and I talked all the way home about school and the changes in my routine. I would have to get up early everyday and get dressed by myself. I would have to pay attention and get my work done at school. I would need to get used to being called "Gloria", which I had never been called. Who knew my name would become a source of conflict between myself and the teacher?

I would be starting school in just a few months now and I was confident that I was ready to be the student and learn from my teacher who I dreamt of all the time now. I wanted my teacher to like me as much as I would like her. I wanted to be a good student and get good grades like my sister got on her report card. It was so much fun getting ready for school that summer. I got to go school shopping for clothes this year and I got to buy my own brand new school supplies! I would get to ride the school bus with my sister and brothers every day! I was so excited when the day finally came and I got to actually go to school.

CHAPTER 2:
SEPTEMBER 1962-

"*I, Gloria ElaineTrujillo,* arrived at the doors of public education brown skinned, Spanish surnamed, female and speaking English and Spanish simultaneously!"

Gloria's journal 1996.

On my first day of school in September 1962, I was awake before anybody else in the house. I was so excited and ready for school! Mom would put a single *chongo*- ponytail pulling the hair away from my face to one side of my head then used water to comb out the rest of my dark brown almost black hair. She kept my hair short because I was tender headed and cried when she combed my hair. I had bangs which she had cut the day before. Mom had put my school supplies in a paper bag and asked my sister to carry them to the classroom. She knew I would probably lose them on the bus. I remember mom was sad as I left for school that morning, she said she would miss my company, we hugged extra long that morning.

Daddy had a lot of advice for me this morning, he told me, "You have to pay attention to the teacher", "you have to behave yourself and not get in trouble", "you have to do what your teacher says to do" and "you need to do your best". Going to school was important in my house because mom and dad did not graduate from high school, they had not had the opportunity to realize their birthright as citizens of this great nation. They expected their children to get up everyday ready to learn at school and get good grades at school. Daddy was the homework parent, he turned on all the kerosene lamps every evening and gathered us at the kitchen table to do homework. He could do easy and hard math with us. He made us read outloud to make sure we understood what we read. I learned a lot sitting and watching dad reteach the lessons from school. By that time of the day, he was very tired from working on the ranch all day and not always patient with us.

"

Today was the first day I rode the bus without mom. Mom and I used to hitch a ride to town to go to the doctor or grocery shop on the school bus. It was so much fun to take the long ride with mom. Mom would send a note to the bus driver who was our neighbor and let him know we would ride in the morning. If I got sleepy, I would use her lap as a pillow and sleep the entire trip home. Today, my brothers had boosted me up onto the bus step which was too high for my short legs. I walked quickly toward the back of the bus to sit with my neighbor who lived in the house across the river. She was sad and didn't want to talk, so I sat and watched the older kids talk. I knew all the kids on the bus, they were my *primos*-cousins *or vecinos*- neighbors. The older kids sat together and talked loud. I remember the older girls combing their hair or putting on makeup on the bus. The bus driver had to tell them to stay in their seats often and to stop moving from seat to seat while the bus was moving.

I walked with my sister off the bus and down the hill past all the other buses. There were alot of kids outside and suddenly I was holding onto my sister's hand tight. I didn't know how to get to the schoolhouse, much less my classroom. I followed my sister all the way to the two story building. Daddy had told me my room would be down stairs, Sally's classroom would be at the end of the hallway and my brother's classrooms would be upstairs in the junior high section. Daddy had explained to Sally that my name at school would be Gloria and not Elaine like I was called at home. She was responsible for walking me to my classroom today and it was important she knew what name to look for on the class list.

My classroom was right across from the secretary and the principal's office. It had two doors, I would learn, one was to go into the room, the other door was to go outside to go to recess, lunch and home. My sister walked me to my classroom and introduced me to my teacher. She had found my name, *Gloria Trujillo, on a* list outside the classroom door. The teacher didn't tell us her name, instead she told my sister to sit me in the chairs against the wall and go to her classroom.

I had dreamt who my teacher would be, I hoped it would be Mrs. Girdano, my sister's first grade teacher. Sally always talked about her as her favorite teacher even now that she was in fourth grade. She said her teacher was nice and praised her school work. Ms. Girdano would even talk to mom and dad at the store and brag about how smart Sally was as her student. I wished my teacher would like me and want to teach me as much as I wanted to learn. I was hoping my teacher would say good things about me!

Now I saw my teacher for the first time and she was a lady in an ankle length dark dress with black heels like my grandma's. Her hair was graying,and in a bun, the skin on the arms hung like grandma's. She didn't talk to us until the bell rang. The bell was so loud, I covered my ears! The teacher walked toward us from her desk across the room. Our desks were in rows facing a large black board, I wondered where I would sit. I reached for the bag of supplies mom had packed for me and waited for the teacher to tell me where to sit. Another student started crying and the teacher moved them to a desk and told them to stop crying.

I watched as the teacher read each name from a piece of paper then escorted each student to a desk. Then I was the only one left waiting for a desk. The teacher came to where I was sitting and told me, "Your name is Gloria and you must answer when I call you." She took me by my arm and led me to a desk at the back of the room. I quickly began to unpack my school supplies from the bag mama had packed. I had a Big Chief tablet, a pack of pencils, a pair of scissors and a bottle of glue in my bag. I could lift the top of my desk and then put the supplies inside, I had watched the other kids do this so I knew what to do.

The teacher took us for a walk inside the building to show us where to go to the bathroom, how to use the drinking fountains and how to go outside to recess. The hallway was wide and there were bigger kids coming out of the doors as we walked by. We had to walk behind the person in front of us, no pushing. Some classroom doors were open and I could see the kids at their desks. The doors to go outside were big and heavy, I could not open them alone! We walked on a sidewalk to another building and went inside. The teacher told us to follow in one line and be quiet. The hallway was full of tall students walking fast out the door, all I saw were legs going by. I would learn that we were inside of the high school which was next to the elementary school. I could smell food cooking and knew we were close to the cafeteria. It was a huge room with tables from one wall to the kitchen. Suddenly I was so hungry just smelling the food!

I was happy when one of the friendly cooks invited us to have milk and sweet crackers. We had to follow in a line to be counted and then we got a tray with milk and yummy crackers! I had never drank milk from a paper box so I did not know how to drink from it. I saw that other kids asked the teacher for help, so I raised my hand and waited. One of the cooks recognized me and came and helped me, she knew my brothers and sister. I had to throw away the milk box and put my plate where they washed the dishes. I wanted to watch the lady wash the plates with water that sprayed but it was time to go.

The teacher lined us up by the cafeteria door and led us out of the building. She took us out to the playground and showed us where we could play and where the bigger students played. I had played here before with my sister when mom and dad went to meetings with teachers. I knew how to swing and ride the merry go round. I was afraid of the big slide because my legs could not climb the steps yet. I watched other kids climb the steps of a big slide then come sliding down fast to the bottom! Then the teacher began to ring the bell she had on her desk. I could see her calling us to her so I ran quickly to get in line with the other students.

When we got back inside the classroom, I needed the bathroom. I walked up to the teacher and tapped her arm and she sent me back to my seat. I didn't understand what she said, but I sat down anyway. I didn't always understand my teacher's spoken words when she gave directions to the class or spoke to me individually. If she called my name to give me permission, I missed it or did not hear her. I wouldn't go to the bathroom until it was time to go eat, then I got to go with another girl.

I was so happy when the teacher asked us to take out our writing tablet and one pencil. I wanted to write on my new tablet! She lined us up to sharpen our pencils but I did not know how to manage or use the pencil sharpener. I was glad the teacher sharpened my pencil as she had for all the other students in class. The teacher asked us to write our first name on a page so I wrote my name, E-l-a-i-n-e, but the letters were big and small. I tried to write it again, as the teacher approached my desk. She took the tablet from me and tore out the page I had written on. She told me, "that's not your name.". The teacher wrote my name as "Gloria" on another page and told me to write it. I got to watch her write the letters one time and now I hoped I remembered. I had practiced writing "Elaine", this was the name my family and cousins called me all the time. Now the teacher wanted me to write this name and I did not know how to write the letter "G". I struggled with the shape of the letter and got really nervous because the teacher was standing over me, waiting for me to make a mistake. This isn't how I learned how to write my letters, mom would guide my hand by placing her hand gently on top of mine. She would help me feel the shape of the letter as we wrote each letter in my name. I would practice writing my name in the air or in the dirt with a stick. I loved writing at home, I would copy words out of the books we had at home just for practice.

Somehow my first day of school was not fun, if school was supposed to be fun. I had sat at my desk all day waiting for the teacher's directions. I had gotten bored several times during the day and found any excuse to leave my desk. I did not answer when she called my name then the teacher would come find me and take me back to my desk. After chasing me down several times, she finally pushed my head down on my desk and told me to keep it down. I didn't like sitting and looking at the floor. All I could see were the top of my desk or my shoes. I wanted to go home.

I was so tired on the long bus ride home, I slept most of the way. I remember my brothers pulling my legs to wake me up. Mom was waiting for us at the stop today, she wanted to know I was okay. She had a lot of questions about the day but when she asked me my teacher's name, I did not know, I called her "teacher". The teacher may have told us her name but I didn't hear it or call her by name.

I awoke early on my own the first week of school because I was still so excited about school! I was learning something new everyday at school, on the way to school and on the playground. If the teacher was mad at me, I missed the cues. Since I was six years old and my first experience in a public school, I did not have prior learning about how teachers interact with their students. I still did not know the name of my teacher while she continued to call me *"Gloria"*. I did not respond every time she called on me or gave directions. I would soon learn the outcomes of my teachers mounting anger with me over these issues.

The day came when I did not come back to class after morning recess and stayed playing outside with my older *primas*. The Teacher sent someone to go bring me back to class and I would be punished for playing too long and not responding when she called for me outside. I did not know I was in trouble until the teacher made me put my hands out in front of her and she hit both of my hands with a ruler in front of the class. I cried out loud because it hurt a lot, she sent me back to my seat to put my head down. When I came indoors, I really needed the bathroom and I asked the adult who brought me inside if I could go to the bathroom first but I was ignored. Now as I sat crying from the pain on my hands, I could not hold the pee and I started to urinate on the floor. My behavior further angered my teacher because now she had to call the janitor to come clean the mess. I got sent to the office to get dry clothes. I spent the rest of the day with my head down. I don't know how I explained the change of clothes when I got home.

I learned that the only time we could go to the bathroom is when the teacher took our whole class to the bathroom right before we went to recess. The teacher would line us up in a single line and lead us to the cafeteria, to the playground and from the playground. She would lead us to get a drink of water. We were not allowed to go out of the room without the teacher's permission at any time.

She taught us a song about birds that we sang while we walked to the cafeteria or during recess. We would get in a single file holding hands with the person in front and in back of us, then drop our hands as we followed the teacher we sang," Fly, Fly, Fly like birds", she would lead us in a snake dance with our arms flapping like birds while we sang with her. She also sang this song with her Mexican servants as she led us off the playground. It looked like a playful game between teacher and students. My older brother would recall seeing our class singing this song on the playground during one of our after school conversations at the table in a joking manner. I laughed along with his story about us flying like birds and mocking our singing. If he only knew where the teacher would take us once we left the playground.

CHAPTER 3:
STOP SPEAKING MEXICAN!

"When English is used to devalue and dehumanize a student who speaks languages other than English, then it is no longer a language of dominance or instruction but a weapon meant to impose inferiority which lasts a lifetime."

- Gloria's journal 1996

I talked in English and Spanish during class because it was a natural method of communication for myself and other classmates in the classroom. In my home, English and Spanish were not separated or segregated, these languages co-existed effortlessly in our conversations. I knew when to speak only in Spanish if I was talking to an elder or the neighbor who spoke only in Spanish. I knew when to speak only in English if I was talking to a person who didn't speak Spanish. I also had the capacity to communicate in both languages simultaneously with my bilingual family. It also helped that I was raised in Trujillo, a small mountain community where the dominant language was Spanish. As children growing up in these homes, we learned to speak both languages simultaneously.

When I started school in 1962, I was introduced to a world where languages are segregated in all content areas. The rule now was to speak English at all times. As I reflect on the impact of this school practice, I see a child who was made to choose one language of learning over another. It's like I arrived with knowledge in two languages but was told that my knowledge in Spanish had no value or place in public school classrooms. I would be dumbed down to one language of learning and be expected to excel at the same level as my English only classmates. I liken my experience to learning with one hand behind my back or with half of my brain.

Being linguistically separated from my knowledge in Spanish was how I learned that speaking only English was smarter and that speaking Spanish was a second class language in the eyes of public school teachers.

When I finished my work, I would tell my neighbor, *"mira"*- "look" at my work. If my pencil fell on the floor, I would go pick it up and tell the other student reaching for it, *"damelo"*- "give it to me". I wanted to always look at their work when I did not understand what to do myself. I would get up from my desk and walk over to other students who were doing the same assignment and watch them, then return to my desk to do my own work. When the teacher caught me looking at their work she would call me a"cheater" for trying to look at their work. She did not understand that I was just checking my understanding of the lesson. I would be scolded in front of class for not doing my own work and made to work alone. I spent many days with my head down on the desk and was denied the chance to check my understanding of the assignment.

I didn't have the words at age six to tell the teacher it was how I learned, I did not want to copy, I just needed another example of how to begin. Instead she had heard me tell several kids at their desks, *"dejame ver"*, which means, "let me see" which angered her that I spoke Spanish in class all the time. She was even more upset with me because she had alerted me by calling my name to go back to my seat and I did not respond again. Now she had to get up from desk and walk over to find me out of my seat. The teacher would grab me by my arm and squeeze while she walked me back to my seat. That hurt a lot! Then as we approached my desk, she leaned close to my ear and said, "you sit down and stop speaking Mexican!" I did not understand what she said I was speaking, I just knew she did not want to hear my Spanish voice. I learned to be very small around the teacher, it was best not to be seen or heard. What was a Mexican? I did not understand the word but I knew it was not good to be called that name by the teacher. I learned that the teacher would get really close to me and whisper that message to me privately, "I said, "don't speak Mexican Gloria!" if she caught me speaking Spanish.

I would watch the teacher go to the chalkboard and write my name in a box with some other names. I came to understand that my name," Gloria" written in that box was not a good thing, I was in trouble. My name was in the box quite often. I did not understand cause and effect therefore I did not stop speaking Spanish during instruction or stop being myself. I came to know the teacher as someone with "mean hands", she pinched legs, pulled ears, squeezed arms and squeezed your hand hard if she was leading you somewhere.

I could not say my teacher's name because it was pronounced too fast and I could not hear all the sounds, so I called her Ms. Overstack, which angered her when I would dare to approach her, her face showed her anger. My teacher was not someone I hugged or whose hand I held voluntarily.

CHAPTER 4:
THE TEACHER' SERVANTS

The teacher would walk us to the cafeteria everyday and be there waiting for us when we finished eating. We would line up and follow her out of the building and onto the playground. She would lead us to our playground area and then release the class to go play. The day came when the teacher did not allow myself and two other kids to go play after lunch. Instead she told us that we were going for a walk with her. I would come to hate the walks with the teacher.

The teacher led us past the high school students playing basketball and all the other kids going and coming from the cafeteria. We walked to a sidewalk behind the high school gym and kept walking. I had learned to follow the teacher and stay in line wherever she took us. I recognized the Post Office when we walked in front of it because I had been there with mom and dad. We turned left at the Post Office toward the store where my *Tia* Rose worked, maybe she would see us walking by. We turned right at the alley behind the store and walked down a dirt road. We finally stopped in front of a large house with lots of steps to climb. I would learn that the teacher lived on the second floor of this apartment building. There was a funny smell, like boiled eggs in the alley, it grew stronger as we neared the apartment building where the teacher lived. As an adult, I would learn that the sulphur smell was a natural hot spring, which warmed the school building and many other facilities in the town, including this apartment building. The climb up the steps was hard for me, my short legs struggled to reach the large wooden steps. I tried to grab the handrail but it was too high for me to reach. The other kids struggled climbing too, instead we crawled up the steps, our hands reached for the step in front as our legs followed. In the moment we were laughing as we tried to race up the stairs to catch up with the teacher.

We finally reached the top and the teacher told us to stand aside because she had dogs. She pulled her keys out one of the huge pockets on her coat. We could hear the dogs barking inside her apartment now as she put the key in the door. She quickly opened the door and caught the two dogs as they ran to her. I had never seen dogs like these, they were the same size with short legs and short hair. Their bodies were long, their ears were large and pointy but they barked loud! She held them in her arms and told us to come inside with her. The door closed behind her and now I was inside my teacher's house.

The three of us stood silently by the door as the teacher walked toward a doorway to the kitchen. I could see a kitchen table and a sink from where I stood. Her apartment smelled awful and I would soon know why. She talked to her dogs in a language other than English or Spanish. Her dogs responded to her commands in that language. Her dogs did not look like the dogs on the ranch; they looked like a weiner in a hotdog! The teacher returned from the kitchen with paper towels like I saw in the bathroom at school but white. She pushed a towel into each of our hands and ordered us to start picking up her dog's poop in the room. I didn't move so she pulled me by my arm and stood me in front of the dog poop at my feet. She pushed my head forward and told me to pick up the poop with the towel. I was then expected to pick up the poop and place the dogshit in a trashcan she carried in her left hand. Once my towel was emptied, I would be directed to another pile of poop. It was a disgusting smell which only became stronger as I squeezed the poop to pick it up with the paper towel These two dogs had pooped all over the floor and behind the furniture.

With three of us cleaning up the shit, the floor was clear of dog poop quickly. We had each been told what to do step by step by our teacher. She also wanted us to wipe the pee they left behind with a paper towel she handed down to us. Now I was directed to go stand by the door and wait. I wanted to wash the dog poop off my hands but the teacher wasn't listening. The other two students joined me as soon as their paper towels were in the trash can. The teacher then takes a clean paper towel and begins to clean each of our hands roughly. She orders us to hold our hands out in front of us as she roughly begins to clean the fresh dog shit off our small hands. Now the teacher wanted us to walk faster as we climbed down the steps holding onto a handrail full of wood splinters. She grabbed the wrist of the student in front of me and ordered us to hold hands and follow her. I had a hard time walking fast and ran into the person in front of me several times. The teacher was walking faster as we neared the noise of the playground. The school lunch bell was ringing and students on the playground started to run to get in line outside of the building. The teacher told us to go to the end of the line and to go wash our hands before returning to the classroom. I could not get the smell of dog shit off my hands after I washed them. Each time my hands neared my face, I could smell the poop I had touched with my hands.

At the age of six I had no concept of days, weeks or months therefore I was unaware of the frequent visits made to the teachers house. I only know I don't want to go there and I become defiant about going with the teacher to her house which ignited her anger with me in class. Sometimes I try to run from her when she meets us outside the cafeteria but she catches me by my arm. The sidewalk was always crowded after lunch with students and teachers walking by on their way to lunch. The voices of students playing and running around drowned out my demands to let me go play.

CHAPTER 5:
THE LITTLE YELLOW SWEATER AND OTHER RECOVERED

Memories

The day came when I wore the little yellow sweater I chose at the big store in Grand Junction when we visited our *primos* before school started. Mom made me promise I would be careful and not lose it at school today. I loved that sweater, it was the color of the sun and I could feel the warmth of the sun on my skin once I put it on! Up until today, mom only let me wear it to church on Sundays, even then I had to take it off as soon as I got home and not get it dirty playing outside.

I got to school so happy and feeling pretty in my yellow sweater! I was extra chatty today and was caught talking during instruction or asking another student what to do. When the teacher asked me to take my work to her, she tore it up and threw it in the trash in front of the class. Without further direction or instruction, I was told to redo my work. She wrote my name on the chalkboard then the teacher made me stay inside during morning recess with my head down on my desk. I couldn't learn the way the teacher taught so I didn't perform well most days.

When it was time for lunch, I ran to the bathroom because the teacher had not allowed me to go during morning recess. I washed my hands and dried my hands, they smelled clean. I was so hungry today and ate everything on my tray. I loved the day the cooks made chili beans and fresh cinnamon rolls, I could smell the food before I got to the cafeteria. Oh boy, everything looks yummy, I was so happy as I sat down next to my classmates to eat. In the cafeteria, I got to sit by my friends and talk to them after I ate my food. I even got to go ask for seconds if I wanted more food. The teacher was not watching me and waiting to scold me in the cafeteria.

It seemed like everyday I made a new friend. Today, I walked out of the cafeteria with my new friend who asked me to go to the swings with her. I was so happy to be invited to go play with my friend, I forgot about the teacher waiting for us outside. She led us back to our playground and released all the students except three of us. She called us back to her and told us to line up, I pretended not to hear her as I ran off with my friend. The teacher called me back and I asked her if my friend could go with us today and she said no and told her to go play without me. I did not understand why she just took the three of us with her on these walks.

I didn't take my little yellow sweater off all morning and I had managed not to get it dirty up to now. During the walk today, the teacher got mad with the boy who always accompanied us because he tripped and fell down really hard. He got up crying because his hands got rocks in them. I watched the teacher grab him by his arm and pull up from the ground. She told him to stop crying and kept on walking. Other adults were driving by or walking by on our walks to the teacher house, but no one asked the teacher where she was taking us. We knew better than to speak to anyone, the teacher was already mad at us.

When we got to the teachers apartment, I took off my little yellow sweater because I did not want to get dog poop on the sleeves and I put it on the arm of the big chair by the door. I had learned the routine at the teacher's house so I waited for the paper towels. To avoid the teacher's mean hands, I would pick up the dog poop before she pointed it out, otherwise she would grab my head and bend it forward toward the dog shit. I came to hate being touched or patted on my head by anybody! Picking up dog poop was disgusting whether it was dry or fresh, the smell was making me gag today and pinch my nose closed. The other girl with us, did gag and almost threw up picking up the dogs shit, but the teacher didn't care, she told her to "hurry up, you're almost done now." There was more shit on her floor today than other days. My hands are so dirty, I can see dog poop on them. I ask for another paper towel to wipe my hands and she gives me one. I now have learned to wipe the dog shit off my own hands and avoid her roughly doing it for me. She is pushing us toward the door to leave and now we are rushing back to school. The teacher walks faster down the long staircase and we struggle stepping down the wide steps. As we walk, we fall down when the teacher pulls on the first person too hard. The teacher does not hold our hands, instead she holds our wrists now, she knows our hands are dirty because of dog shit picked up inside her house.

When we got to school, she sent the three of us to wash our hands. The soap and water did not get rid of the smell on my hands anymore. I spent the rest of the day trying to learn with the smell of dog shit on my hands. I wondered how others did not comment on how I smelled or perhaps that is why I sat at the back of the class. I still did not miss my little yellow sweater when we reached the school but I did miss it when it was time to go home. I did not remember where I had left it or maybe I didn't want to remember going to the teachers house. When I got home after school, mom asked me for my little yellow sweater and I didn't know where I had left it. I was so sad that I had lost the sweater the first day mom let me wear it to school.

The next day I would go look for my sweater on the playground, in the lost and found and the hallway where the big kids hang their coats and sweaters. I even asked the teacher if she had seen my sweater and she only shook her head from side to side. That day after lunch, the teacher hurried us to her apartment as usual. I wish she would let us go play like the other kids. As soon as I walked into her house, I saw my little yellow sweater on the floor. The dogs had used the bathroom all over my beautiful sweater, I told my teacher, "looky teacher, it's my sweater!" She said, "you left it here." I wanted to take the sweater with me but she would not let me. I began to cry out loud now which angered her. No matter, she shoved paper towels into both hands and ordered me to begin cleaning like the other classmates who had come with us. Why was my teacher so mean? Why did the teacher hate us so much? Why couldn't I take my sweater home? I had a lot of questions at age six but no answers.

The loss of my little yellow sweater stayed with me for sometime. I was confused about whether I should tell my parents it was at my teacher's house and she wouldn't give it back to me. I was afraid my parents would not believe me and then take me to see the teacher who would be even meaner with me at school. So my parents were never told about the little yellow sweater or the visits to the teachers house.

Picture Day

My first picture day at school was special for me, I would wear the dress I wore for my first Holy Communion on Easter Sunday that Spring. It was a beautiful white dress with a big skirt which made me feel so pretty! I think it was the dress my sister wore for her first holy communion but it was new to me! Mom had curled my straight hair with bobby pins and put my favorite hat barrettes in my shiny black hair. I wore the same white shoes and socks to match that day, my feet had grown and they were tight on my feet but I wore them anyway. This was a special day and mom wanted me to look my best. When I got to school, I had to give the teacher the money envelope for the pictures. I could hear the teacher telling other kids how nice they looked. One boy had a suit on and the teacher told him he looked handsome. Another girl had a pretty red dress on and the teacher told her she looked beautiful. When I got to the front of the line, the teacher reached for my picture envelope and told me to sit down.

I remember going to take my picture, and the photographer did his best to get me to smile, but it was hard to smile with the teacher standing next to him. He was friendly and joked around with us to make us smile. I had become used to not smiling in my teacher's presence after the visits to her house. Sure enough, after lunch, the Teacher did as she always did: walk the class back to the playground from the cafeteria and take her Mexican servants to her house. Oh if mom only knew I would be picking up dog shit in this white dress and stepping in dog shit with my pretty white shoes by lunchtime!

1st Parent Teacher Conference

At the first parent teacher conference, mom went to my conference and Sally's. Dad went to my brother's conferences upstairs. I was not allowed to go inside the classroom with mom, I had to sit outside the classroom and wait quietly. From where I sat outside the door, I could hear what the teacher was saying about me. The teacher did not have good things to say about me, she told mom I was too social, that I did not respond to my name all the time and that I did not get my work done correctly. She went so far as to tell mom, "Gloria talks too much Spanish at school and it does not help her".

Mom stopped asking questions after the teacher said that to her and the conference ended. I didn't get any A's on my report card, instead I got S minus and NI- Needs Improvement. On the way home, mom told dad what the teacher had said about me and that she did not like my teacher's message or her behavior. *"Esa es una mala mujer"/"* She's a mean woman", my mom would comment. Oh if they only knew how mean she was with their baby girl!

My parents didn't scold me after the conference or tell me to stop speaking Spanish at school. They did tell me I was too social and needed to stay in my seat to finish my work. I love that my mom and dad did not punish me for speaking Spanish because it came so easy to me! It was the way we lived and learned English and Spanish at the same time! Thanks to mom and dad, I grew up respecting two languages in my lifetime!

The Christmas Program

The teacher announced that our class would be singing songs for the Christmas program! I was so excited, I loved to sing! I sang with my family at home and in church. I knew how to sing Christmas songs in English already. This was going to be so much fun! Then the teacher announced we would be singing Christmas songs in German because she didn't know how to sing the English songs. That was when I realized the words she used with the dogs at her house were German. We spent many hours learning to sing "Silent Night" and "Oh Christmas Tree" in German. I could mimic very well and pretended to sing along as best I could. The teacher made us repeat the words over and over again, she wanted us to say the words correctly. The tune of the songs were familiar but the words were so hard for me to say. The teacher loved teaching the class to sing in German, she seemed really happy at school these days.

The day of the program came and my parents drove me to the program that evening. I had told them about singing in German and about the songs our class would sing. I went to join my class behind the stage and wait for our class to perform. The teacher called me to her side and told me my job would be to hold the curtain open for the other kids when they sang. I would not sing with my classmates, instead I was a prop which held the stage curtain open and off the stage. I sang anyway, hoping mom and dad could hear me. The people clapped really loud when our class sang for a long time. Our class and the teacher bowed then walked off the stage. Another boy and I held the curtain until all our classmates were off the stage.

Mom and dad loved the program and the songs our class sang even though I was off stage. They didn't ask why I wasn't singing with the class, I guess they were happy I held the curtain. I loved singing along silently to the songs the other classes sang, like "Frosty the Snowman", "Jingle Bells", "Deck the Halls", "Away in a Manger", and "Oh Little Town of Bethlehem". I had learned the songs from my brothers and sister who were in 4-H and went Christmas caroling in our community every year. Oh the fun we had, our neighbor who had a team of horses and a large sled, we would go from house to house picking up our neighbors to go sing songs at the next house up the road. It was so much fun! Mom and Dad would go along and we drank hot cocoa from a thermos bottle they brought along to keep us warm.

I loved the days it snowed a bunch because the teacher did not take us to her house on those days. I also loved the days the Teacher was absent. There were a lot of snow days where I lived! The teacher had to stay at the school during lunch and have the classroom open for the other students who could not play outside because of the snow. I was so happy to be able to stay inside and play with the Lincoln logs, jigsaw puzzles and building blocks. I loved being able to play with my friends! Most days I was not allowed to play with these toys because my work was not acceptable to the teacher.

CHAPTER 6:
THE TUMMY ACHES BEGIN

After Christmas vacation, I didn't want to go to school anymore. My parents thought it was because it was cold and I just wanted to stay home with mom where it was warm all day. At the age of six I learned that staying home with mom was safer than going to school, this pattern of behavior will follow me into my career as an educator. I developed tummy aches at home and at school which were often ignored by mom and dad when I told them. My tummy aches were real, my tummy would knot up just thinking about returning to the teachers house, her dogs and her treatment. At age six I felt alone with my secret. A secret I shared with two other classmates. All those days we walked together to go work in the teachers house and we never spoke of those days as children. It will be another 50 years before we find each other and talk about 1962 for the first time as adults. The child who started school with gusto and a positive attitude had changed.

Mean Math lessons

I came to hate math lessons with the teacher because I got scolded and berated during her one to one time with me. She would insist on adding and subtracting on an abacus which conceptually I did not understand. The color of the beads represented parts of the math operation and I was to use one color for each addend and another for the sum or total. I had already learned base ten math and could add and subtract to twenty with ease by the time I started first grade. With the teacher at my side, I would be dumbed down to counting by ones a color at a time while she slapped my hands if I reached for the wrong color. I would get so nervous with the teacher who I did not trust or like, I looked dumb in math.

It was my daddy who taught those math concepts at home. I was raised on a sheep ranch and my job at age six was to count the sheep and lambs as they walked through a wooden shoot. I was too small to count them inside the shoot so I stood at the end of the shoot and counted out loud starting with one and going past 100 sometimes!

I had watched this process from the time I was a toddler and learned to count by mimicking my siblings. Now I had to be able to recite the numbers in correct number order, this was a very important job I was doing! Daddy had paper and pencil to tally my count, I watched as he drew four slash marks and then joined them with a fifth that went across them. He could do that really fast! Then he drew a circle around two groups of five to make a group of ten. He then counted by tens to get a total count of the sheep and lambs. He then switched jobs with me and made me do the slash marks in groups of five and then make them into groups of ten. Daddy was a good math teacher and I learned how to add and subtract with base ten before I was in first grade. My teacher did her best to convince me otherwise, in her eyes I was weak in math. I would come to believe that too for the rest of my life! I was more successful with the math workbook, I knew how to read math problems because I watched my sister do her homework. I loved to get A+'s on my workbook pages and would take those home to mom and dad.

The duties of lunch time servant continue

As the winter progressed, I grew to hate the walks to the teachers apartment after eating lunch. I wanted to be like the other kids and play on the playground after lunch with my classmates and cousins. I got to be a normal kid during morning and afternoon recess which I enjoyed every minute. I learned how to climb the ladder up the big slide and how to play hopscotch with the bigger girls! I loved to play "not it" with the kids which meant I ran a lot during recess. The teacher on duty would ring a bell she carried with her and the fun would end. I loved being outside more than being in the classroom.

The walks to the teachers house were harder now with the snow, icy sidewalks, muddy back alley and slippery steps to climb once we got there. I remember falling down many times, only to be pulled up by my arm quickly and hurried along. My hands were full of mud or ice by the time I got to the other job of picking up dog poop. I wished the teacher would let me wash my hands with warm water so they wouldn't hurt and maybe I could pick up the shit easier. The teacher hurries us along once she pushes a paper towel into each hand. She orders each of her three Mexican servants to an area of the living room and kitchen where the dogs stay during the day. The door to the bathroom and her bedroom remain closed, we don't clean in there. I quickly go looking for dried shit first because it's easier to pick up with the paper towel and I can get rid of it faster. It's the fresh poop that I hate to pick up, as soon as I bend down to try to pick it up, the smell hits my nose and I want to pinch my nose closed. Then I remember that my hand is dirty but I have already pinched my nose. I hate crawling under the kitchen table to get the poop but the teacher demands that I do. Now she washes our hands off with a wet paper towel which takes off more of the poop but not the horrible smell of dog shit. This is a dirty job I do for my teacher and I don't know why.

As an adult, I have developed the habit of smelling my hands after I wash them, and if they smell sour or the towel is used, I will rewash them and use a clean towel. Sometimes, not even a clean towel will do. I will simply wash my hands with soap, rinse, and use a paper towel. I smell every kitchen or bath towel before I use them to this day. If they smell sour or like ammonia, I will use another one. As an adult, I will never have a dog as a pet because I never wanted the responsibility of cleaning up after them. I still find the smell of dog poop repulsive when I smell it on a dog trail. I realize now that once diagnosed with PTSD, a service dog would have been so helpful to me to keep my anxiety and emotions in check at school.

I had learned the routine of returning to the playground after walking back or running back to the school grounds from the teacher's house. When we got to the post office we slowed down because there were a lot of people going in and out the building. Some talked to the teacher as she walked by with three students following behind her. Now we cross the street and we are behind the high school gym and we can hear the bell ringing marking the end of our lunch recess. The teacher wants us to run now, but the sidewalk is icy and hard to walk on. She walks away from us now as if we are no longer together. The three of us know the way alone and find our way to the end of the class line. The teacher stands outside the classroom and waits as we go into the bathroom to wash our hands. She inspects our hands today as she has other days and makes the boy go rewash his hands again. All the soap in the world can not erase the smell of dog shit from my hands and my nose, it stays with me inside the classroom.

It is not until the afternoon recess that I finally take a deep breath of fresh air and run to the playground where I am free to play with my classmates. I am still the social and playful kid I have always been when I am with my *primos* and classmates. I join in the playground games in progress such as hopscotch or jump rope. I loved it when my *primas* in the older grades turned the jump rope, they turned it slowly so I could jump in and jump with a group of girls. That was so much fun! I loved playing chase now that I could run up the big slide and slide down without falling.

Inside the classroom I was a different kid, I had learned to avoid the teacher inside the classroom which was easy because she did not spend much time with me. I learned to keep my head down when the teacher confronted me about talking in class and not responding to her. I became sneaky about looking at my neighbors work so I knew what to do. I learned to whisper and be secretive with other classmates, especially when using my Spanish voice. I had learned to survive in the teacher's classroom and avoid her wrath. After lunch, I was still her Mexican servant along with my other two classmates until the last day of school.

CHAPTER 7:
THE LAST DAY OF SCHOOL: BURN IT ALL!

On the last day of school, mom sent me to school with a large brown paper bag from the supermarket. She told me to put all my school supplies inside the bag and bring them home because today was the last day of school. I don't know that I understood my own joy at age seven, but I did understand I would not have to return to the Teacher one more day!

The last day the Teacher took us to her house, we got splinters on our hands from the hand railing going up the steps. I cried because it hurt alot when she pulled them out of my hand. The wood was dry from the hot sun now and the splinters stuck to our hands as we reached for the handrails. Once we got inside the house, the three of us quickly picked up and cleaned up the shit on her floor. She had taught us to wipe the floor with a wet paper towel if there was a fresh shit left behind. The teacher was standing above us with a roll of paper towels ordering and directing us to clean us after her dogs. The teacher would pull out the splinters out of our hands before we got back to school. The steps are still hard to climb even though we have all grown this year. Today the teacher gave us a popsicle to eat on the step outside her house, I got a red one. It tasted so cold and delicious, I forgot all about the splinters and so did the other two kids.

The last day of school, I got out of school after we ate lunch. In the morning, we emptied our desks and cleaned them inside and out. I had to erase all the pencil marks on the desk and inside of my reading book. I got to play outside for a long time this morning. I remember the teacher lined us up to walk us out to the bus on the last day, some kids were crying and sad when they hugged the teacher and said goodbye. I was not sad nor do I remember hugging her the last day or any day.

I got on the bus and found an empty seat all by myself. The other kids on the bus were laughing excitedly and cheering about it being the last day of school. They reinforced for me the fact I would not be returning to the teachers class again. Some of the kids had already thrown their leftover supplies in the trash before they got on the bus and announced they did to all of us. The bus ride home was always long and most days I slept or visited with my neighbor who was in my class. She was one of the three kids the teacher took to her house most days. We never talked about the visits to the teachers house even though she had gone with me all year. I kept it a secret and I guess so did she.

I am so glad I am sitting alone today, I hug the paper bag full of leftover school supplies to my chest and rest against the bus window. I look outside but my mind is busy thinking about what I will do with the supplies I am holding. There are no trash cans at my house to just throw the stuff away. The memories of the teacher are in this bag I am holding. The pencils I chewed in class when I did not know what to do, the mathwork book which reminded me of the painful lessons with the teacher, the unfinished work I did not turn in but hid in my desk and the pictures I colored or drew but never showed the teacher. I further rationalized my thoughts with, "I don't think mom and dad will ask me to show them my papers on the last day of school", so I gave myself permission to get rid of them.

When the school bus stops, we still have a long walk home. We could not use the log bridge now because the river was too high and dangerous to cross. We got off with the other kids at the bus stop and we walked with them until the road turned off to our ranch. I hug the paper bag to my chest, careful not to let anything drop. I usually run to keep up with my brothers and sister but today I am not afraid to walk alone as I usually am. As they run ahead of me I am walking and thinking. I knew that our family burns the trash outside in the arroyo because I help haul stuff there myself. I knew that mama grabs wooden kitchen matches from a striking box by the wood stove. She makes a pile of trash in the middle of the arroyo where there are no weeds or sticks to catch fire. We fed the leftover food to our dog or saved it in a barrel for grandma's pigs so this was just paper and boxes that we burned out doors.

As I near our house, I climb the short trail from the road to our house. I had watched my brothers and sister run in the front door and disappear. I decided to go in through the kitchen door where I knew mom kept the matches. I left my bag of papers outside and walked into the kitchen. Mom is talking with my sibling at the table where they are enjoying a delicious bowl of freshly cooked chile beans. No one noticed me come inside and grab the matches. I quickly walk out of the kitchen and close the screen door quietly. I grabbed the bag of papers and headed for the arroyo behind the *comun*-outhouse. I walked up the arroyo to a burn spot where I know it's okay to burn trash. I emptied the bags of papers on the ground and grabbed the loose paper and put it on top of the math workbook. Now I will try to light the match, the way I have watched mom and dad light them. I squatted down on the ground and grabbed a rock I can hold in my hand easily. I pulled a wooden match from my pants pocket and struck the red end on the rock, it broke! I got another match from my pocket and struck it on the rock, I saw sparks but it did not light! I got another match from my pocket and struck it firmly on the rock, it lit this time! I put the match close to the papers I put on top of the pile, the paper started to burn! With my small hands I fan the flames hoping the other papers would burn. As the paper starts burning, I feel happy as they disappear in a pile of ashes. I want all of them to disappear along with the memories of Ms. Overaker, it's taken this long for me to mention her by name. I don't call her "my Teacher" somehow I know she has not earned the title. I watch over my fire, pushing the math workbook pages toward the flames. These pages are harder to catch on fire so I opened the workbook and began pushing each page toward the flames, its working the book is on fire! I stand up and watch as the smoke begins to lift high in the air and I am happy watching the pile go up in smoke and slowly disappear in a pile of ash. I begin to dance around the fire taking quick side steps while fanning the smoke over me. I skipped and ran around the fire as it burned, producing more smoke as it grew and rose higher and higher in the sky.

19 F's and 24 A's

My mom has sent my brothers to go look for me because I have not come into the house. I am an easy find, they see the smoke from my fire and come running to see what I am doing. By the time they arrived the fire was burning hard, the loose papers had all burned along with the pencils and crayons. The only thing burning was my math workbook. My brothers did not ask what I was doing, instead they started to stomp out the fire and throw dirt on the flames. My workbook got kicked out of the fire to one side and I ran to pick it up, I did not want them to see it. It was still burning, and I couldn't even go near it. My older brother stomped out the flames with his shoes and picked up the workbook.

I don't remember the dialogue I had with my brothers that day, I do remember the feeling of dread I had for them finding me. Neither of them asked me why I was burning my school work at the end of the year. Instead, they assumed I was hiding bad grades and such. If they only knew, I was hiding a huge secret I thought I could resolve on my own at age six.

Now my oldest brother starts the painful counting of the grades left in the workbook out loud! I kept jumping up trying to take the book away from him but he was taller than I and I ended up crying when I could not take the book away from him. When we got back in the house, I was crying and angry with my brothers for having stopped me from burning the workbook. The badly burned workbook was kept as evidence of my actions on the last day of first grade. My oldest brother would report to my family that I had 19 F's and 24 A's in the workbook which was true.

The story about the fire I started on the last day of school became one retold and shared with cousins and neighbors. Little sneaky Elaine had tried to hide her failure on the last day of school by burning her books in the arroyo. I hated that story because it was not the truth, it was simply another low expectation of my success at school. I felt a lot of shame for the whole first grade experience then which I carried internally into adulthood.

At the age of six , my coping strategies for dealing with the shame of first grade were limited without advocates to speak on my behalf. At the time, I felt I could not confide in anyone in my family. I was sure they would not believe what happened to me all that school year. Instead I decided the best thing was to pretend nothing happened. I would become the kid who masked her pain in different ways. I cried easily, angered easily and took playful pranks personally. I had learned to cope with my teacher's abuse by avoiding her at school and not drawing any attention. I learned to be sneaky and to avoid eye contact with adults when being disciplined. I had also learned to make excuses to stay home where I felt safe and avoid school completely.

"Children Learn what they Live"- Poem
Children Learn What They Live
Dorothy Law Nolte - 1976

If a child lives with criticism, he learns to condemn.
If a child lives with hostility, he learns to fight.
If a child lives with fear, he learns to be apprehensive.
If a child lives with pity, he learns to feel sorry for himself.
If a child lives with ridicule, he learns to be shy.
If a child lives with jealousy, he learns what envy is.
If a child lives with shame, he learns to feel guilty.
If a child lives with encouragement, he learns to be confident.
If a child lives with acceptance, he learns to love.
If a child lives with approval, he learns to like himself.
If a child lives with recognition, he learns that it is good to have a goal.

If a child lives with sharing, he learns about generosity.
If a child lives with honesty and fairness, he learns what truth & justice are.
If a child lives with security, he learns to have faith in himself & in those about him.
If a child lives with friendliness, he learns that the world is a nice place in which to live.
If you live with serenity, your child will live with a peace of mind.

With what is your child living?

This poem I carried through my whole career in public education. I still remember receiving this poem as an undergraduate student in one of my first teacher education courses in the 70's. I can remember the professional dialogue associated with this lesson, it was meant to help prepare future teachers for the fact that every child comes from a home which is functional or dysfunctional. This poem helped us novice educators to understand the long-term effects of parenting in the lives of our students. I would post it on the bulletin board closest to my desk where I could read it easily and refer to it as needed.

Today it's a validation of my experience at school. As teachers we are in "loco parentis", which means in place of the parent. This basic educational foundation concept I understood clearly as a budding educator. As a student in first grade, I was trapped in my teachers house against my will and forced to learn oppression and racial discrimination at age six. I surely learned what I lived in first grade 1962.

"Real education should consist of drawing the goodness and best out of our own students: Cesar E. Chavez.

CHAPTER 8:
LEARNING TO BE A STUDENT IN 2ND GRADE

As the summer came to an end and the talk about school starting soon began, I started to have tummy aches at home again. A familiar burning right under my rib cage that came on as soon as I went to bed and caused me to sleep in a fetal position, holding my tummy. The kind of pain that worsens with anxiety and the unknown. I had constipation issues because the anxiety I felt would literally stall my digestive process. I still suffer the same way to this day when my anxiety is heightened.

I remember being so afraid that I would be reassigned to the Teacher again. I was afraid to even see the teacher much less be her student again. Daddy had a meeting with the Teacher before the end of the school year who made him doubt my readiness for second grade. According to her, I had not grown academically as I should have after nine months of school. My daddy left the meeting without accepting her decision for retention.

I would begin the school year unsure of what to expect from my new teacher, I had lots of questions and drove my mom crazy with questions about the new school year. I was so anxious about starting the school year, I finally found the courage to ask about who my teacher would be. Mom would let me know I would get a new teacher because I was going to be in 2nd grade now. Yipee, I was not going to be in the teacher's class this year!

On my first day of second grade, my sister took me to my new classroom across the hall from my old classroom and further down the hallway. My new teacher is standing outside the classroom greeting her students. My new teacher was young and very pretty, she had brown hair combed like the older girls on my bus. She wore glasses and had on earrings and a necklace that matched the dress she was wearing. My sister and I approached her and the teacher said, "Welcome to second grade, you must be Gloria!" How did she know my name? My teacher had a picture of me in first grade on the card she was holding. I was completely surprised when she reached out to hug me then she took my hand. This was my first hug from a teacher at school, it felt as warm as mama's hugs. She asked my sister if I rode the bus and the bus number so she would know what bus line to find me in at the end of the day. She told my sister her name was Mrs. Fortenberry and she would be my second grade teacher. I was surprised when she walked me to my desk and introduced me to the other students in the class. She told them, "boys and girls, this is Gloria and she will be in our class this year." The kids that were at their desks waved at me and said, "Hi Gloria!" Some of the kids who had been in my class last year, I recognized their faces and names. The teacher had written my name on a paper with a big smiley face and placed it on the desk I would sit at.

I unpacked my supplies carefully and quietly, a Big Chief tablet for writing, a pack of unsharpened pencils, a box of crayons and a ruler. The girl who sat behind me wanted to ask me a question but I was afraid to answer because I thought the teacher would get mad. Instead, I put my head down on my desk and sat quietly waiting for the teacher to tell me what to do next. I did not want to get in trouble on the first day of school! I noticed that the other students were visiting with each other as the teacher greeted each of her students and walked them to their desk. She squatted down to visit with her students and answer their questions one at a time. I had no questions for my teacher because I did not know what to ask or how to ask her so she wouldn't be mad.

I finally found the courage to ask her if I could go to the bathroom after I saw other girls ask her and be allowed. I waited until she got back to her desk and then I asked for permission. The teacher allowed me to go but I had to wear a bathroom pass that was like a necklace around my neck she had made just for the girls in her class. I put the necklace on with the pass to the front and went to the bathroom. I knew where to go by myself. As I stepped out in the hallway, I froze because I realized that I would have to pass in front of my old classroom, and I was afraid at that moment. Just the thought of seeing my first grade teacher made me walk very fast past the door that was closed. I was so sure she was still in that room and that she would come and take me to her house again! I used the bathroom and washed my hands and stepped back out into the hallway. The fear gripped me as I found myself running past her door even though I knew there was no running in the hallway. It was no surprise when another teacher walking into the office next to the bathroom, told me to walk back to class. I was so glad to be back in my new classroom.

As I reentered this classroom, I noticed it was bright and had a lot of color on the walls. The teacher had the blinds open to let in the light and she had the lights turned on all the time. This was not like my old classroom where the teacher hardly ever turned on the lights, the room was as dark as her house. Now I am in second grade and the teacher knew we could read so she put our schedule on the chalkboard and explained all the subjects we would study every day. We would study reading and math in the morning and all the other subjects after lunch.

I already liked my teacher's smile, she was friendly and explained things to us patiently. I understood everything she said and it felt so good! What was the same this year was that my teacher did not speak Spanish so I would be separated from my home language at school again. I had learned that when your teacher does not speak Spanish then I could not speak, read, write or think in Spanish during instruction. I would be expected to learn in English only during school hours for most of my elementary school years. It was like learning with half of my brain, the one with English thought and knowledge.

Our class practiced lining up for recess and lunch then she took us on a walk to show around the school. Our class would play on the same area of the playground as in first grade. This year, I could get myself in and out of the low swings without help! I could climb up the big slide and climb the monkey bars all by myself, it was awesome! Our teacher rang the bell she carried in her hand. Then she took us to the cafeteria and we got a snack from the friendly cooks.

Our teacher talked with cooks about having cold milk brought to our class as a snack in the morning and what time she would send students to get it from the cafeteria. This was a new routine for this year. Last year only some of the students in our class got milk and the teacher decided who based on our behavior. Maybe this year was going to be better because the teacher was different.

As we re-entered the building to go back to our classroom, our class passed the first grade classrooms on the right side of the hallway. Now the door to my old classroom was open and suddenly I froze in place, the student behind me nudged me to keep moving. I did not want to pass in front of the open door because I was sure the teacher would come out and claim me again. I had to keep walking and was so relieved when I saw a different teacher come out of that room! I continued to stare at her and wondered if she was visiting the room or if she was the new teacher.

Once we got back into the classroom I put my head down on my desk and sat quietly. The teacher noticed me sitting quietly and approached me. I was scared for a moment, until she spoke, "Sweetie, are you feeling bad, why is your head down?" I wasn't sick, I was feeling anxious about seeing my old teacher. I didn't answer her, instead I sat up like the other kids and asked her what I was supposed to do now. I was so unsure about how to behave in this class and with my new teacher.

The first time I was called to the reading group, I was scared and nervous because I was sure I would be scolded and bullied for not being able to follow her teachings. It happened with the other teacher and I remembered that moment. I sat quietly as another girl began to read out loud, the teacher liked the way she read and told her so. Another boy was called to read out loud and I read along with him silently. When she called on me, I stumbled to get started and she helped me by reading along with me. I was surprised that I was able to read along with her easily! But wait, that is how I read with mom and dad at home and at church. I recognized my own ability to read at that moment. I felt good about myself when I left the group and I came to have many of those moments in second grade.

Everyday was an opportunity for me to show my teacher how smart I was and that I wanted to learn more from her. She was the kind of teacher that celebrated the little things we did. I remember clapping along with her when a student got an answer correct or reached a goal in a subject. The first time the class did that for me, I was so happy and speechless! The walls were covered with our success stories.

I loved seeing my name on papers with A+ hanging on the walls, it made me feel so special and smart. It was the little things my teacher did to let me know she cared about me, her student. I learned so much about being a teacher from my second grade teacher, I will never forget the little things she did to make her students know their value as human beings.

When lunch time came, I would still expect the teacher to be waiting for me to go on a walk to her house. I remember being so anxious during lunch in second grade until I got used to the teacher escorting our class back to the elementary playground and releasing all of us to go enjoy our recess. It didn't take long for me to love lunchtime recess. I had made lots of friends in class because being social was natural to me but this year it didn't get me into trouble with my teacher. I loved being able to be a student like all the other kids and being able to play freely as they did. I loved being in 2nd grade!

I remember the Valentine party and the fun we had getting ready for the class party. I would learn how to decorate a small box with the red, white, pink crepe paper and as many construction paper hearts as I wanted to paste on it with love words. On the day of the party, the teacher gave each of us a special valentine and a heart shaped cookie to enjoy. She told us we were all her "special valentines". She gave the best hugs and held our hands gently if we were the class line leaders.

In second grade I learned to be creative and expressive as a student. I learned how to talk to my teacher and ask for help without fear. I learned how to show my teacher I was learning when she asked. I knew she would not be mad when I made a mistake or didn't know the answer correctly. I was a totally different kid in class that year!

By the end of 2nd grade I had made significant progress in all content areas. I was reading with confidence and understood when asked comprehension questions. I had overcome my fear of math lessons once I watched my teacher help a boy who could not add or subtract. She was patient and gentle with her words as she explained the process to him. I knew how to add and subtract so I was hopeful my teacher would be happy with my progress.

After second grade, I would progress through elementary school and middle school with minimal symptoms of trauma. I still held back and would let someone else respond in class though I knew the response. I carried an inferiority that could not be explained and baffled my dad, who often told me, "You have to believe in yourself above all others." I was an average student with A.B and C grades in any grading period. I did not test well and never felt the test reflected my knowledge of the content. In high school, I was popular and visible. I was a varsity cheerleader, a class officer and Spanish club president. I kept a B average so I could participate in extracurricular activities like cheerleading and pep squad.

As a sophomore in high school I was recruited by a Talent Search project who visited our school on a monthly basis. My high school Spanish teacher, Mrs. Marquez, encouraged me to attend these meetings because she knew I was planning on going to college after high school like my older sister. I was so happy to have two Spanish surnamed recruiters helping me with college applications and applying for financial aid which I would have struggled with on my own. I did not relate to their knowledge of the Farm Worker movement going on in California or the identity "Chicano" which they used comfortably. However, It will be my mother's connection to Farm Work that will ensure I have a path to college.

At the end of my Junior year, I was accepted to Adams State College and received a financial aid package for the first year of college! I was so excited to tell my parents who did not have the means to send their youngest daughter to college. My mom had helped me qualify for a Farmworker grant because she had picked crops in the San Luis valley as a teenager and lived the life of a field worker sleeping on the ground in a horse stable with no restrooms and one source of water shared by all the pickers.

Now all that was left to do on the college application before I returned it, I needed to get a signature from the high school counselor whose office I had never visited. I took the application and stood outside her office waiting to be invited inside. The school counselor reviewed my application while I chatted nervously about my college plans. Imagine my shock and surprise when she looked up from the application and told me to my face," Gloria with your attitude, aptitude and grades, you will never make it in a four year college, I would suggest cosmetology." Her comment was so hateful, I responded back with, "Fuck you, I don't need your help!" and I grabbed the application out of her hands. Of course I paid the price for being a disrespectful student! I was sent to the office and made to call daddy who had to come to school. This was the first time he had come to school because I was being disciplined. Daddy made me apologize to the counselor for my bad language, who sat behind her desk arms crossed and stated, "I don't know what came over Gloria, it's not like her." This counselor did not know me though I was a visible and active student. The high school principal signed my college application so I could complete the college prep process. Meanwhile, the high school counselor got away with being racist and rude. I will always wonder how many more of my Spanish surnamed classmates got those same discouraging words from this counselor.

On the long drive home dad talked to me about the counselor's behavior more than mine. Somehow he understood my frustration and anger with her response to my request for a simple signature. He would tell me, "Sis, there are people who you do not share your dreams with because they don't believe in you."

"I've learned that people will forget what you said, people will forget what you did, but people will never forget how you made them feel."

Maya Angelou

CHAPTER 9:
WELCOME TO TEACHER EDUCATION! - SY 1974-1977

"If the student doesn't learn the way you teach, teach the way the student learns."
Dr. Helen Gonzales: Bilingual Professor

As a college student at age 19, I was a part of a special opportunity in my undergraduate program, a bilingual elementary teacher internship program. I would learn to teach effectively in two languages, English and Spanish. This was a dream come true for me, an opportunity to use my bilingual skills in a classroom! I had never abandoned my Spanish voice despite the 2nd class treatment in public schools.

This was the decade when Cesar Chavez's struggle for farmworkers unleashed a lot of grant money for Mexican American students to be recruited to area colleges. I had been recruited by a Talent Search program as a sophomore in high school. With these funds came the opportunity to recruit bilingual teachers to serve communities with high migrant populations. I was on my way to fulfilling my dream of becoming the teacher who would embrace bilingualism in her classroom with acceptance and respect.

One of my college professors at Adams State College was Dr. Helen Gonzales, who had a single metaphor displayed at the top of her chalkboard constantly, "If the student does not learn the way you teach, then teach the way the student learns." Which means that if a student does not learn in English, then teach in Spanish. Through her teachings, I learned to teach, organize, plan and deliver instruction in English and Spanish to students whose home languages were other than English. I could totally relate to this approach because it was the way I learned and lived.

I loved the bilingual education classes provided within this internship, *"Canciones del pasado"*, *"Literatura Infantil"*, *"Estudios de matemáticas, ciencias y estudios sociales"*. Which meant I received these subjects in both languages simultaneously in the same classroom. As a group, we were bonded by the focused education classes we received in two languages. My professors were skilled bilingual educators who trained fourteen bilingual teachers over a two year internship.

"How Dare you Speak that Language"
- 5th grade teacher

As I progressed through my bilingual internship, I would become more confident about speaking Spanish in school and around other teachers in our program. This took some getting used to after years of English only learning environments. I also became more confident as a teacher when presenting instruction in English. I would find out that the public school communities where we would complete our student teaching experience, were not informed or educated about the bilingual interns who would be on campus for the next three months. We were placed into the same English only system we had grown up in as children.

I would be assigned to do my student teaching in a rural school community about fifteen miles from the college. I was assigned to a second grade classroom and carpooled with other interns in the program who were psyched about completing our student teaching experience and beginning our careers as bilingual educators.

The day came when I was preparing to teach a Spanish science lesson and my cooperating teacher suggested we go practice the lesson in the teacher's lounge. I collected the felt board and the handouts I would need for the lesson and followed her upstairs to the teacher's lounge. I had developed and cut out all the felt pieces for this presentation which were popular visual aid teachers used in the 1970's. There was a full size couch and several arm chairs in the lounge. I decided to set up my materials on the couch where I could set up my felt board. I had not noticed the teacher who entered while I was setting up, she took a seat in one of the arm chairs out of my view. I began to practice the science lesson dialogue out loud as I placed the parts of the plant on the felt board. My students were expected to respond to my questions in both languages without conditions about language mixing.

"Yo digo, tu dices." - *I say you say.*

Esta es una hoja verde. - This is a green leaf.

Este es la rama de la planta. - This is the stem of the plant.

¿Cuántas hojas tiene la planta? - How many leaves does the plant have?

Meanwhile, my back had been turned away from the teacher who had entered after us, now she was pacing back and forth in a small area. I kept on with my Spanish practice lesson when all of sudden she was standing in front of me. From where I was seated, I could see she was wearing a dress with heels. I looked up at her as she began to speak down to me in a loud angry voice, "How dare you speak that language when you know I don't understand!" Her face was red and the veins in her forehead were raised, the pointer finger of her right hand was in my face. I was stunned for a moment before I chuckled and responded from where I sat, "How long have you lived here?" The teacher responds, "All my life!" To which I responded, "You have lived here all your life you haven't learned any Spanish from the people around you" My statement only angered her and as she turned to leave the teacher's lounge, she stated she was on her way to the principal's office, "We'll see about this!"

My cooperating teacher scolded me for my response, she told me I was disrespectful to a veteran teacher who had a lot of influence over the principal. She actually told me, "Gloria you cannot talk to *gringos* that way, you'll get in trouble." A *"gringo"* in this context refers to a person who only speaks English.

I would learn that the teacher and principal were both Mormons and members of the LDS church who had religious and economic power in this community. I was now very concerned about my student teaching placement which could be terminated, or I could be reassigned to another school community which would be embarrassing. I was even more concerned about how the director would respond once he knew what happened in the teacher's lounge. I would have to wait until Monday to learn my fate from the building principal.

As you can imagine, I agonized over this incident the whole weekend. Once again, I felt the shame of being a Spanish speaker in a public school system. I felt ashamed for how this woman had confronted me inside the teacher's lounge. Her face and her anger are familiar to me. I had seen and heard this kind of anger from another teacher at school when I was in first grade after she heard me speak Spanish.

On Monday morning, the principal asked to see me privately in his office. I was scared to hear the outcome. He had been friendly and welcoming up to now, but all that could change now. I entered, sat down and listened while he talked. I was so relieved when he told me he had not contacted the director of the bilingual internship program at Adams State. Instead, he had made the executive decision to ban me from the teacher's lounge and I was not to speak Spanish in the hallways. I was also to avoid contact with the veteran teacher who had been offended by my behavior.

I would not tell any of the student teachers or my husband what had happened at school, I was too embarrassed and ashamed of myself to speak of the event. While I could have confided with the other interns in the group, I don't recall talking about this event with anyone. I was so afraid of the repercussions and what it would do to my career. I stuffed the event into the far corner of my memory and pretended nothing happened

However, I never forgot the shame I felt as an adult when I was punished for speaking Spanish at school again. I did such a good job of pretending nothing had happened, that eighteen years later I would return to this same elementary school as their principal!

Meanwhile, I began my teaching career in 1977 as a bilingual resource teacher in a district with a 95% Hispanic student population. This school district was the perfect start to my career in education and I am grateful that I had this experience before entering the world of general education teachers. I was responsible for teaching Spanish language arts and social studies in English to intermediate elementary students. I worked alongside gifted Spanish surnamed teachers who used both languages in their teaching methodologies constantly. I loved the opportunity but the commute to and from home was two hours! Two years later I accepted a job in an agricultural community with a large migrant population not far from where I was living. This would be my first experience as a general classroom teacher responsible for all content areas in English.

CHAPTER 10:
THEIR HANDS ARE THE COLOR OF DIRT! –
1979-1986

It was in this school district that I experienced the "triggers" associated with having PTSD for the first time. I would witness the attitudes and treatment of Spanish speaking students only to trigger my own delayed trauma unknowingly. I would not make any connections to my own trauma for many years. I would eventually shut down, become disconnected from my work and resign a tenured teaching position. My family did not understand what happened to make me leave a good job and the brand-new home my husband had built for our growing family. I would not understand my decision to leave until I got into therapy at age 65.

The fact that I was the only Spanish speaking teacher on the second-grade team meant many of my students were from Mexico and their parents were harvesting crops or working in potato cellars. I also had the local Spanish surnamed people with generational roots in the town, many of whom worked in the same cellars sorting potatoes. As their teacher, the Spanish dominant speakers in my classroom were not deprived of their brilliance in Spanish as I had experienced as an elementary student. Instead, I accommodate their learning needs by allowing them access to their primary language through my instruction therefore I taught the way they learned. I had few if any anglo students in my class and of the few, several would choose to move their children to a monolingual classroom because of my use of the Spanish language.

The day came when two of my migrant students in second grade returned to the classroom with their hands bleeding during a lunch recess. I was in the classroom grading papers and getting ready for their return to class. When they walked into the class, their hands were dripping blood on the floor. I quickly got up from where I was seated to assist them at the small sink in the classroom. I could see the fear in their eyes when I asked them what happened to their hands then in their dominant Spanish voices they began to tell me what had happened to them:

La señora Green nos llevó a su clase a ayudarnos con la lectura y cuando entramos a su clase nos dijo que teníamos que lavarnos las manos antes de usar sus lápices. Nos llevó al baño y con un cepillo muy duro nos lavó las manos y ya ve nos salió sangre. Entonces nos mandó con Usted.

After I had stopped the bleeding by applying gentle pressure to their small hands, I sent them to the nurse for larger bandages than I had for them. I was hoping she would investigate but I knew the chances were slim because she did not speak Spanish and would not be able to understand how their injuries occurred.

Meanwhile, I was angry at the teacher who had injured two of my Mexican students. I made the decision to advocate for them by going to the source of their injuries, Ms. Green, the Special Education teacher. Now mind you, these migrant students were not in Special Education therefore not her students. She took it upon herself to go out to the playground and take these innocent boys to her classroom. Of course, they went willingly, they had no reason to question her intentions, she was a teacher at their school!

I walked into her room and up to her desk. I stood in front of her and asked her, "What happened to Noel and Martin's hands? They returned to class with their hands bleeding from your classroom." She looked up at me and calmly told me, "Gloria have you seen their hands, they are the color of dirt! I simply helped them clean up because obviously their parents don't care." I could not control my next action, I took my hands and opened them in front of her face and told her, " my hands are the color of dirt like theirs, do you want to take a brush to mine too?" To which she replied, "Oh Gloria you are taking this way too personal, I was helping them I said". At that moment I wanted to slap this woman as hard as I could, but I knew I would face the consequences not her. She would be protected at all costs and I would be fired for assaulting her!

I made the decision to report the incident to the building principal who was new to the community and to migrant students. I waited until I calmed down before I went to see him about the incident. I would retell the incident from the moment the students returned to my classroom with their hands bleeding to my going to Ms. Green's classroom to confront her. I was shocked into silence and shame by his response to the violence this teacher imposed on these students. He told me, "First of all Ms. Lopez, these students are not the kind whose parents come to school, so you need not concern yourself with them. Secondly, your job is to get along with Ms. Green, after all you are her colleague. Now is there anything else I can do for you Ms. Lopez". I left his office feeling ashamed and insulted at the same time. What could I do? These families did not have telephone access working in the fields, so I would have to contact their employers who would not release them from farm work. If I pushed the issue with the employer about the abuse to their children, these parents would have lost their job. I also knew the employer would report the issue to the school and get me into more trouble as well. When a migrant student gets sick at school, they often stay in school regardless. They cannot go home because mom and dad are out in the field or in a cold cellar sorting potatoes. I would learn that the school had a migrant liaison person who could have intervened and helped me with this matter but I was a new teacher and did not know about this resource.

What the principal did not know was that on the first day of school that year, I had Ms. Green demand I give her my seat during the first general meeting because she felt entitled to it. She had come and tapped me on the shoulder as I visited with my teaching team at an assigned table on the first day, then stated, "I need this seat and the aides stand in the back." I tried to ignore but she was persistent. After disrupting me three times, one of my colleagues spoke up and told her, "This is Ms. Lopez, the new second-grade teacher". I however, turned to the back of the room to see two beautiful brown skinned females with long dark hair like mine, standing against the wall. I would introduce myself to them and learn they were teacher assistants who worked in the primary classrooms. I would come to respect them as teachers, friends and neighbors once we got to know one another.

Within the next school year, my husband and I planned to start our family. My pregnancy was easy, I was so healthy and free of morning sickness. I would say my only side effect was my huge appetite. My oldest son was born on Christmas day of 1981. It was such a joyous time in our lives after my mother-in-law passed away a month before his birth. I had a lot of support from my teachers during this time, they donated sick days so I would not be docked pay when I ran out of sick leave. I experienced postpartum depression after the birth of our son which I attributed to the fact I had a C-section and was forced to return to work before I healed internally. My husband was unemployed at the time so returning two months after his birth was the only financial choice I could make.

I would learn in EMDR therapy that I was actually starting to shut down and disconnect from my job after the incident with Ms. Green and the principal. I remained a teacher in this same district for another six years and pretended that nothing happened to my Mexican students though I had witnessed the violence personally.

I found that ignoring and avoiding racism became an exhausting practice for me in this school district the longer I remained a member of this staff. I remember sitting in the teacher's lounge with my colleagues, all anglo and hearing one of them read the headlines from the local newspaper out loud, "A Van full of Mexican Nationals, illegal aliens were stopped and deported outside of Monte Vista read the headlines. "Well it's about time they do something about these people coming here to drain our country of resources meant for citizens" The teacher reading out loud would realize that I was sitting right by her so she put her hand on my knee and told me, "Oh but not you Glory, you're one of us!" It was her way of rationalizing her racist comment. Meanwhile, I had to sit in silence and allow this racist comment to go right by me.

After the birth of my second son, I was transferred to a pre-first classroom. It was not a good move for me to try to teach the grade where I had experienced a massive amount of trauma as a child. That year, I was absent more than the previous year. I found myself wanting to stay home more often, now mind you I had two babies at home now and went to school exhausted most days. Then I became disinterested in my work at school, I did not want to be there anymore. I remember standing at the window of the round shaped school I was teaching in and dreaming of being anywhere except where I was at that moment.

I could understand my behavior or my decision to resign my position in 1986 without notice to my family or my colleagues at school. I will not understand or process the PTSD symptoms I was experiencing while a teacher in this school district for many years. Meanwhile, I immediately have to find another teaching position elsewhere. Once I resigned my teaching position in this district, I regained my confidence to market myself again and started applying for jobs.

CHAPTER 11:
FALL- 1986: THE TUMMY ACHES RETURNED IN MY CHILDHOOD ELEMENTARY

These school memories were hard to contend with in my therapy because I had carried so much shame, guilt and denial for how I exited one school district only to return to my hometown as a 3rd grade teacher in the fall of 1986 and quit! I never talked about this teaching experience to others and never included it in my resume. I would quit 45 days into my contract because my health deteriorated physically and emotionally in that time period. I had just resigned a tenured position abruptly only to return to my hometown thinking things would be different for me somehow. At the time, I had no recall of my childhood trauma, but I was symptomatic, nonetheless.

Through my therapist and my own research on the subject, I learned that childhood trauma is a psychological injury which has longstanding and chronic effects on adults. Adult survivors of complex childhood trauma can struggle with processing what they survived in childhood, which can lead to a host of emotional, psychological and physical symptoms. The unresolved childhood became PTSD symptoms which I could not always hide from family members or employers. I also learned that my unresolved childhood trauma also limited my abilities to venture into schools or new places. Instead, I would return to the very school districts where I had previously acquired the trauma. I will do this twice in my career. This was so hard for me to comprehend as an educated female, it made me feel so stupid for thinking things would be different once I returned. My therapist helped me to understand I also returned to the sources of my trauma because I wanted to heal and resolve the trauma subconsciously.

I had accepted the job in my hometown in 1986 because my husband had been offered the opportunity to set up a Talent Search project in the area. These educational projects had been instrumental in recruiting both of us to college as high school students and now he had the chance to direct his own project. It was a great opportunity for him at the time. I would interview for the 3rd grade teaching job at the elementary school and accept the job as soon as it was offered to me. My husband could not move with me immediately because his transfer had not been finalized. Instead, I moved the 90 miles back to my hometown with our toddler sons without him! It was so hard to leave my spacious house and get used to living in an apartment by myself with two toddlers. I was lucky to find a relative in my hometown to care for our babies as soon as I relocated. My parents had been caring for my kids since they were infants and were now dumbfounded about why I moved and took them away from them.

From the very first day back in my hometown elementary school which was now a new building, I began to experience the same tummy aches I had in first grade. The same dull ache right below my rib cage and radiating to my whole belly I thought was stress, lack of sleep, fatigue and anxiety from living as a single parent with toddlers. I suffered the tummy aches night after night without making any connections to my childhood trauma. Instead, I learned to sleep in a fetal position with a hot water bag which meant my sleep was disrupted when the bags leaked and wet my bed. I thought I was experiencing stomach ulcers and soon realized I could not stay in this situation all school year by myself. My husbands' transfer never materialized and I was left to make the decision to resign my position as third grade teacher and return to our home.

I remember the day I went to see the superintendent of schools who I knew personally, he had grown up in the area and now was the superintendent of schools. When I entered his office that day, the tears began to flow voluntarily. I felt so much shame for leaving my students at the end of the first quarter and felt so much guilt for the decision I was about to make. Between the tears, I explained the situation with my husband's transfer and how unlikely it was he would join me any time soon. He was very understanding of my situation and understood my leaving. I would not talk about my own health issues, I simply resigned and returned to our home without a job. My tummy aches stopped the first night I returned home, it felt so good to sleep through the night pain free.

Within two weeks of returning, I got another job twenty minutes from our home. I was still a very marketable teacher with ten years of experience. I was hired as a fifth-grade teacher to finish the year for a teacher who had been reassigned to another position. I had a hard time adjusting to teaching two different grade levels in the same school year which meant more planning and materials development. By the end of the school year I informed the principal I would not return even though I did not have a teaching position.

CHAPTER 12:
ONTO TO GRADUATE SCHOOL- 1988-1990

At this point in my career, I felt "my well of learning was dry". I felt bored in the classroom and wanted something different. I would tell myself, I needed to go back to school and re energize my career with new learning. My husband was in favor of higher education and supported the idea of us going to graduate school in the northern part of Colorado. This would mean relocating our family and renting our home for the time being. My parents were heart broken when they learned we would move far from home for several years while we acquired our degrees. They loved taking care of my babies and I knew it was going to be hard to not have them close. I soon learned, it was hard to trust strangers in large cities with the care of my children, not to mention the cost of good childcare. I would teach another two years at a community school with a 95% Spanish surnamed student population in overcrowded classrooms. Meanwhile my husband earned his Master of Arts degree in vocational rehabilitation counseling at the University of Northern Colorado in Greeley.

I would attend graduate school at Colorado State University in Fort Collins, which meant we would relocate that summer and live in a townhouse next to the football stadium. I was accepted into graduate school that fall and registered for classes in the Educational Leadership program. I also landed a job with an alternative teacher certification project for secondary teachers. I would supervise student teachers in the field who already had a BA but had never taught in a classroom. It was a great opportunity for me because my intentions were to earn a Type D certificate so I could become an elementary principal upon graduation.

I was super busy being a graduate student, working part time and being a mom to elementary school aged boys. Our weekends were spent on soccer fields watching our boys enjoy a sport together. I often took my kids to class with me as a graduate student when I had no one to leave them with before my husband got home. They would sit at the back of the classroom and play with their action men while I participated in classroom dialogue and work. The highlight of my masters studies were the classes with Dr. Faustino "Chuck" Luna, he taught courses in Multicultural Skillfulness. His teachings helped me to understand and recognize the nature of prejudice and how it manifests in the belief systems of others. His favorite statement was, "behavior is a function of what people believe", therefore racism is a visible and measurable behavior in society. His definition of what it means to be different in America I would share with students and teachers alike as a school leader; "different is just different, it's not better or less than, it's just different." I conceptualized this to mean that as human beings, we are not math symbols, we're not greater than one another, we're not less than one another, we're not even equal to one another, we are just different from one another. I often used math symbols when presenting this concept in a classroom setting.

My graduate program passed quickly and before I knew it, I was at a crossroads between taking a principal position that fall or continuing my studies as a PHD candidate. I would complete my master's program in December and graduate with a 3.86 grade point average. I felt proud of my academic accomplishments and was being groomed to enter the PHD program by two of my professors who I trusted and respected. I decided to begin my PHD program when the semester started after Christmas break. I also continued my principal internship at an area elementary after graduating because I had wanted to continue learning from a very progressive principal who encouraged me to stay on as a volunteer until the end of the school year.

The semester began and I quickly adapted to the rigor of a PHD program and my work at the elementary school. I was the sole Hispanic female in my PHD program and shared a graduate office with several PHD candidates. I knew many of the candidates already because we had classes together with the same professors. I had six or seven professors who taught the masters and PHD courses which meant the content would be different, but the instructors would remain the same.

CHAPTER 13:
"THIS IS THE PRICE WE PAY FOR AN EDUCATION" - CSU UNIVERSITY PRESIDENT-

As a PHD student, I would be assigned to work on class projects with other candidates. I enjoyed meeting a PHD student named Ed who was a former coach for a USA Martial Arts Olympic team. Ed was just weeks from completing his PHD program and graduation, this was his last semester. As a speaker and presenter in class, he was motivating, energetic and prepared. I enjoyed his participation in class and got to work with him on a class project that semester. This was the reason I was in the graduate office waiting for him to get out of class that day so we could work on our project together.

I was sitting at my desk in the graduate office and I could not see the door from where I was seated because there were filing cabinets blocking my view. All of a sudden, the door flies open and it's Ed like I have never seen or heard him before. He takes his books and slams them down on a table close by. He begins pacing the floor and yelling loudly "What the fuck?" "What just happened?" "What brought that on?" I am taken back by his behavior because he's taken off his belt and his shoes. I am so thankful we are the only students in the graduate office that afternoon. He continues his rants out loud. "What's this nigger shit, I thought we were way past that shit!" He begins to walk toward the door muttering that he wants to go hurt them! No doubt Ed could have <u>done</u> permanent damage to the alumni professors upstairs. I then began to try to defuse the situation and keep him from doing something he would truly regret, like beating the shit out of an old man! I finally asked him what happened, and he turned to face me. He then started to cry, I was shocked to see the tears streaming down his face, but he began to tell me what happened.

He had been the last one to leave the classroom that day and as he left three of the alumni professors who taught the afternoon courses were standing outside the elevator talking together. This was a usual occurrence every day between classes. The professors would stand outside and draw candidates into their conversation at random. On this day Ed was walking out and headed for the elevator when one of the professors called him into their circle. Without any reservation he openly states to the other two alumni professors, "This is one of the few good niggers we have at CSU!" Even though these professors were hearing impaired, they all heard his comment and began to laugh. One even patted him on the back! Ed was shocked into silence and could not respond. He quickly got on the elevator and had come to the graduate office where I was expecting him.

I did not want to believe that such a racist comment had come out of one of our professors, but I had reason to doubt Ed, who was a black man. I told him repeatedly not to act on his instincts and report the matter to the "higher ups". I validated his anger over the racist comment and told him I understood what he was feeling because I had a similar experience myself outside that very elevator. I reminded him of the fact he would go to jail for beating up these old guys and never see his family or graduate. I told I would go with him as a witness and advocate.

The next time I saw Ed in class, he was wearing sunglasses which he had never worn in class before. I sat next to him and realized he had been crying based on the track marks on his face. He was silent during class, which was so unlike Ed, he was usually an active participant but not today. We met after class and decided we would report the incident to the President of the college. I called and made the appointment for both of us to meet with the President in his office the following week.

Ed and I met outside his chambers and spoke briefly. I expected Ed to do most of the talking and I would be there to support him. However, the dynamics changed when the President, also a black man, invited us to speak freely as PHD candidates. Ed spoke highly of his PHD experience and the value it brought to his life until the day in front of the elevator. As he began to retell the events of what happened and what was stated by his alumni professor, he became emotional and choked up. It was so hard for him to tell the President of the university, he had been referred to as "one of the few good niggers we have at CSU." His tears ran voluntarily. The President sat in silence and asked me why I had come to see him. I stated that I was there to support and advocate on Ed's behalf. He then asked if I had experienced racist comments from these professors and I answered, "yes". Up until this moment, I had not talked about my day in front of the elevator to anyone, not even my husband. I had pretended nothing happened, it's how I had coped until this moment. He then asked me to retell my experience.

This incident took place a week or two before Ed's experience while we were both candidates in their PHD program. I had attended two classes back to back and was in a hurry to go pick up my kids after school as class ended. I packed up my school bag full of books and headed for the elevator. Three of my professors were standing just outside the elevator as I approached. They were engaged in a conversation with another student, and I walked around them on my way to the elevator. Just as I approached the elevator, one of the professors invited me into their discussion by saying, "let's ask Gloria her opinion." I don't remember the content of the discussion or what I was trying to say exactly. All I remember was being in the middle of a sentence when the professor who invited me into the conversation interrupted me, after I pronounced the word "because" as "pecause", accidentally. Now, he is looking down at me and saying loud enough for many to hear him, "you still don't have a handle on this language, do you?" My teacher was doubting my ability to speak English based on my mispronouncing the word "because." In the moment, I was shocked into silence and did not respond to his racist comment, instead I disappeared onto the elevator as their laughter filled the foyer. I never spoke of this incident until that day in the President's office when he invited me to retell the racist comments I had heard.

As I finished retelling the incident, he asked both of us how close we were to completing our PHD programs. Ed and I answered separately. The room became silent as the man behind the desk sat in silence as if thinking about what he would say next. His next statement shocked both of us. He looked at us directly and told us, "That is the price we pay for an education." I could not believe this man was identifying with us on one hand but not at all surprised by our experiences in front of the elevator. He didn't even want to know their names or the classes these professors taught. I remember responding, 'that price is too high for me." In the next instant, he excused us by saying, "Is there anything else?"

We walked out of his office silent. There were no handshakes or expectations for successful completion of our PHD program. We were simply dismissed.

I quit my PHD program the second he spoke those words to me. I was immediately on a flight out of there, I had no fight left in me that day. I don't remember processing the experience with Ed after the meeting. We both continued with our studies as best we could. After that, I would see Ed wearing sunglasses in the classroom.

I immediately lost interest in my PHD studies. I was disgusted by the fact that at least three of my seven professors had displayed racist attitudes toward Ed and I. Those facts were hard for me to ignore thereafter. I had a major internal conflict going on in my head. I did not want to learn from these professors one more day, because I no longer valued their knowledge on any level.

Over the summer months, I decided to leave my PHD program and seek employment as an elementary principal. Ed and I would never speak again about this incident. I always wondered if Ed completed his PHD program and went on to mentor students in his hometown. My world became more complicated by this incident, I wanted to quit my program and had lost the desire to earn a PHD degree.

"I'm afraid you will lose faith in a system you are very qualified to be a part of" Jaime Escalante- Stand and Deliver

CHAPTER 14:
MY FIRST JOB AS AN ELEMENTARY PRINCIPAL

Up until this point in my life, I had dealt with trauma simply by removing myself from the school setting or pretending nothing happened. Despite the fact I was carrying baggage from many unresolved school traumas which had mounted since age six, I was still a marketable and effective educational leader. That will all change with this administrative assignment. Before I accepted this job in the fall of 1990, I had been offered three different principal positions in the Denver metro area for twice the salary of the job I would accept. I turned them all down for the opportunity to move "back home".

When Tomas and I left for graduate school four years earlier, we intended to return to our home in southern Colorado after graduating. Tomas had built our beautiful home from scratch during a period of unemployment. We had made the adobe bricks with our hands which were used in the construction of the home, it was beautiful! Tomas did a lot of the construction himself, so he had saved us a lot of money. The San Luis Valley was also where our aging parents lived.

When my sister informed me of the principal position opened in the district she was employed in, I decided to apply for the job. This elementary school was the very same school I had completed my student teaching in some 18 years earlier, this fact will come back to haunt me. At the time, I was thinking this was our opportunity to return home to family and our home. My husband did not want me to take this job, he wanted to remain in the northern region of Colorado. We had purchased a second home in Fort Collins while I was in graduate school and had made a comfortable life for ourselves. However, after I quit my PHD program, I wanted to leave the area immediately. I was still in "flight mode" and traumatized by the visit to the president's office.

Once again, my husband and I will live separately for the first year of my principalship because he has not found employment in the area. This will only add to the stress of being principal and single parent during the school week. I doubted my decision to return but kept telling myself things would work out for our family. There were signs this may not work out, but we made it work somehow.

I would be offered the job over three other candidates with administrative experience. At the moment, I was happy and excited to be returning to the area close to family and familiar surroundings. Our boys would grow up close to grandparents and cousins. At this elementary school, I would be their principal, and I would be able to visit them in class and have lunch with them! I loved visiting their classrooms and watching them learn and grow along with their peers and cousins. They would get to visit me in my office after school. It seemed like the right career choice at the time and for the first three years, it worked!

Within the first nine weeks of my principalship I had to deal with a male teacher being fired for breaking into the home of one of our teachers and robbing her of her safety and privacy. He had stolen keys to her house the previous school year and knew where she lived because he had been there before. On this particular day, the kindergarten teacher was at home sick and he had taken personal leave to perform this criminal act. Imagine my shock when the teacher called to tell me of the arrest at her home that morning when he had walked into her house and she was home! I called the superintendent to inform him of this matter. The outcome of this event will haunt me as this teacher supervisor and colleague because this teacher became a liability to this district the minute she called me to report the matter. I will face the same scrutiny when I report violence in this district four years later.

As the principal I would have to comply with the superintendent's expectations. The teacher was fired immediately after the arrest but he requested a letter of recommendation from the district before resigning. I was given the task of writing the damn letter which was four sentences long and said nothing about him as a teacher. The word got out to the teacher that I was writing a letter of recommendation for the man who had violated the privacy and safety of her home and work and I lost her respect at that moment. The teacher never returned to her teaching position and I would rehire another teacher to finish out the year. I never forgot this teacher's creative force in the classroom, she was vibrant and animated in her delivery of instruction. She was a determined kindergarten teacher who simply reported the violence and abuse of a fellow co-worker. She didn't deserve what happened to her and I always hoped she continued her career in education at some level.

For the first three years of my first principal assignment, I loved the work I was doing in this elementary school. The Hispanic superintendent who hired me was supportive and pleased with my work as an administrator, I was professionally satisfied as well. I would apply the "shared leadership" principles learned in my principal internship with the staff in the school. Unlike top-down leadership models, shared leadership empowered teachers to take an active leadership role in running the school. I had a strong team of teacher leaders in this small school who had a mission and a common goal driving their efforts as teachers. Within three years, we had returned all our special needs students to our elementary school using a Full Inclusion model in our Special Education program. We now had students with Down syndrome, Fragile X syndrome and wheelchair bound students enrolled in our small rural school. At the same time, we developed a gifted and talented program which partnered teachers with parents in this after school program. Our tiny rural school competed with schools in the Cherry Creek school district in Denver in an annual competition of gifted minds called Destination Imagination while I was principal of this school in 1992-1994.

In order to accomplish this school wide mission and goal, we partnered with the Board of Cooperative services who provided professional development and additional Special Education support staff to our school. The director of Special Education had taken a special interest in our school and often participated in the day-to-day operations of our Full Inclusion program. He had been supportive of the accommodations we were able to provide our special needs students.

During my third year, the superintendent announced he would retire at the end of the school year. I was sad to hear of his decision because we had a positive and professional relationship which had allowed me to thrive and grow as a principal. By the end of the school year, it was obvious the school board was grooming the principal of the high school to be the next superintendent of school. With this transition in power came the beginning of the end of my career in this school district.

CHAPTER 15:
THE CHANGING OF THE GUARD: SETTING THE STAGE FOR VIOLENCE

As the new school year began that year, a different tone was being set by our new superintendent. He had been my colleague for three years and now he was my boss! I had learned a lot about his background before the formal interview for the job. He was proud to admit he was "grandfathered" into his principalship without having to do an administrative internship. His lack of leadership development will soon be my demise. He was more social and on friendlier terms with members of the school board which played out in school board meetings. The personal agendas of school board members began to set a tone for zero tolerance of students they believed were "gang members". The student population profiled as "gang members" were from a small predominantly Spanish surnamed community about nine miles from the schools.

With a zero tolerance mindset, out came the" flicker board", a paddle meant for corporal punishment, it was about an inch thick and had several large holes drilled into the paddle shaped board. It also had the words "Flicker Paddle" painted on one side. The term "flicker" referred to the mascot this community had for their winning Catholic high school basketball team in the 1960's. This smaller community school was forced to consolidate with the larger neighboring school district once their school closed.

The principal of our son's middle school was now walking the hallways of his school with the "flicker board" in his hand. At home, we had been informed of how uncomfortable he was when the principal approached his classroom, slapping the board on his thigh where he read the words "flicker board" written on one side of the paddle.. He had classmates who recognized the stereotype meant for their community and had educated him on the message behind the "flicker board" paddle. My husband attended the Parent Advisory Council meetings where he advocated for our son and those students who felt threatened by their principal's racist behavior. He would also visit the principal in his office and demand he put the paddle away.

My husband's participation in the PAC meetings was not popular with some board members. While it was his right to advocate for our son and the students being threatened with this paddle, he was now an enemy of the school board. As his wife and an employee in this district, I was now being looked at differently. The issue divided the community, you had those who believed these students should not be allowed to continue their education in this school and those who advocated for their children's safety at school.

With the change in leadership also came a different attitude from the Special Education director who had a special relationship with the new superintendent and the board members. This would play out during an early morning Special Education IEP meeting in our school. The meeting was set for 7:30 a.m., the superintendent of schools would attend this IEP because district policy called for the presence of the superintendent if the IEP included a need for student transportation. I made the decision to begin the IEP even though the director of Special Education who was not yet present to allow the teachers to return to class. We had completed introductions of the team which included the foster parent, the SPED team from the student's school and our team. In total about ten people were in attendance that morning. Just as our SPED teacher and general education teacher began to speak, the director of SPED showed up late to the meeting.

He had issues with us starting without him and he made it known to the team. When our teaching staff continued their line of questions to the SPED team from the student's current school, he became verbally aggressive. This man who had worked alongside our staff for two years suddenly was acting aggressively toward two members of my teaching staff. He had a chair with wheels and made use of such a function as to pull himself up to the table and in the face of our SPED teacher. I had never seen this behavior from this man in the two years he had worked alongside our staff. He would tell her, "The problem here is you and your principal, you just don't want to work with this Mexican student!" I intervened immediately and said to him, "if you have a personal issue with myself or Ms. Hamilton, this is not the meeting for that." I did not get to finish my statement because in a flash he was in my face. Keep in mind that my boss, the new superintendent, is witnessing this whole scenario and remained quiet the entire time. The Director of Special Education is now in my face yelling at me, "Don't you attack me Mrs. Lopez", he got nose to nose with me and I could not ignore the intense smell of alcohol on his breath as he yelled at me. He quickly withdrew and wheeled back to his place in the group. Meanwhile, I was shocked into silence and had to remove myself from the meeting. I was so glad the playground was empty because I needed some fresh air. I began to walk the perimeter of the playground on this brisk fall morning without feeling the chill in the air. The fact that this professional showed up to a meeting in our school intoxicated was serious to me, his aggressive behavior toward two of my teachers was serious to me. As their immediate supervisor I knew I was responsible for their safety in the workplace therefore I could not ignore or pretend nothing happened. Before returning to the IEP meeting, I went to my office and reported his aggressive behavior to his supervisor, the Executive Director of the San Luis Valley BOCES- Board of Cooperative Services.

The director came on the line, and I began to describe the scenario at our early morning IEP meeting in progress. When I informed him about the smell of alcohol on his director's breath, he remained silent. I was once more shocked into silence when he responded with, "Gloria I am not going to reprimand him, you need to learn to work with him after all he spends more time in your school than others, you should be thankful." Before I could respond, he hung up on me! At the end of the meeting, I informed my boss who was present during this meeting that I had reported his aggressive behavior to the executive director. He told me that was "unnecessary" in his opinion and that I should not have so without consulting him first. Opps too late.!

I returned to the meeting and the transition process for this student was completed which was the goal of this meeting. Meanwhile, I have two teachers who are traumatized by the action of the intoxicated Special Education director during this IEP meeting. Above all else, they want to know the conditions he would be allowed to return to our building in his capacity.

I knew I would have to request a meeting with the goal of resetting boundaries with our teaching staff and this would not be an easy meeting. The meeting was set for November 30, 1994 at 2:00 pm at the San Luis Valley BOCES. Until ten o'clock that morning, the superintendent had me believing we would drive up together to this meeting, then I got the message from my secretary that I would have to drive myself to the meeting because he had an earlier appointment.

CHAPTER 16:
NOVEMBER 30, 1994
A PROFESSIONAL RAPE-I SAID "STOP MANY TIMES

"Behavior is a function of what people believe"
FC Luna- Graduate Studies Advisor

Today was daddy's birthday, November 30th so before I left for work, I had called him to sing a few verses of *"Las Mananitas"*, a traditional Spanish birthday song I had learned as a child. At the end of our conversation, daddy told me, *"Siempre bendita de Dios mija."*, which means "Always in God's blessing, my daughter." I will cling to these words as I drive into the parking lot of the building. My gut instinct is already alerting me to the danger ahead.

It is a cold November morning, and the parking lot is icy as I carefully make my way to the door. I am clutching a manila envelope in one hand which contains the agenda for the meeting. I make my way to the receptionist desk who gives me directions to the Executive Director's office. She then calls his office to let him know I arrived. I find the hallway to his office and begin to walk toward the door. A small window in his office opens to the hallway so I can hear male voices speaking inside. I recognized three male voices immediately. I hear the Executive Director say, "So how are we going to play this?" The Director of Special Education responds with, "Well, she asked for it." While the Superintendent of schools, my boss responded with, "Let's do this", followed by a collective power clap. By then my presence is sensed and they make their way into the hallway where we meet. Today, there are no friendly greetings amongst colleagues and I realize I am about to enter a meeting with three angry males! These licensed school officials will redefine the term "gang rape" with their titles within the next two hours! I will have a different perception of the "gang issue" in this district because I had become a target in this school district!

We entered a conference room which had been closed and is not heated for this scheduled meeting. It's freezing cold in the room by design and I do not take my coat off! I enter the room to find a single large conference table filling the room. I followed my boss to the right side of the table and sat next to him. The Executive director sat across from us and the Director of SPED sat at the head of the table with the door behind him. Once the door closes, I feel trapped!

The Executive director asks if I bought an agenda for the meeting since I requested the meeting. I acknowledged by handing him copies of the agenda I had prepared. He read over an agenda and then stated, "You are expecting way too much!" as he handed a copy to the other two males. The room silenced for a few seconds then the Director of SPED began to speak. His body seemed to take up the entire space at the head of the table with his posturing. The assault began.

He started with, "Nothing happened at your school, you made the whole thing up." From this point on, he's the only voice in the room. He points his right finger at me as he speaks and sits straight up in his chair. His legs are squarely on the floor. I didn't know this man felt so much hate for me until that moment. His berating continued with all his statements beginning with the word, "you".

"You are the neediest principal I work with, constantly needing support and affirmations."

"Your teachers think you are a joke, and I hear about it all the time.

"You are pathetic always asking for input from your teachers."

"Your teachers don't like you like you think they do!"

"You give yourself too much credit as a principal."

"You can't even get the name of the school right!" (I pronounced the school name in Spanish as written- "*La Jara Elementary*")

"You think you are some kind of Chicana leader, you're not."

I looked right at him and stated, "This is about you, not me!" after each of his statements and he talked right over me! It's at this point that I know I am in trouble. I speak to my boss directly sitting to my left and I tell him, "Stop this meeting now."

I am ignored. I pulled on his blazer sleeve and repeated my statement, "This meeting is over! "He does not respond. I looked at the Executive director who ignored my requests by acting like he did not hear me as well. These two professional white males condoned his behavior with their silence and allowed the verbal assault to continue.

Meanwhile, the Director of Special Education continues his abuse of power over me. He now knows I have no support in the room, and he has permission to continue his assault, as his words continue to express his disrespect and hate for my gender and leadership. He becomes more animated in his delivery, after all he had an audience! He now has one leg crossed over his knee which is in motion, his right hand busy at his groin area. He catches himself and pulls his hand away, but he can't leave it alone. I recognize this man is sexually stimulated by the power he has been given by the two silent white males in the room. He knows he can say and do as he likes. I am disgusted because what is happening is completely against my will. His voice fills the cold room and I continue to beg the meeting to be stopped only to be silenced by all three males.

I have fleeting moments when I think about jumping out of my seat and running for the door but what if they tried to stop me. I thought about walking around the table and kicking this man in the head, the one between his legs doing all the thinking!
Instead, I stayed until the end.

When he ran out of English words, he would throw out vulgar Spanish words like, "You're just a puta from the 70's raising hell in this district!" It seemed like forever before my boss finally speaks, he says, "Ok" and gives a time out signal as if he's coaching a high school wrestling match! I immediately spring up from my seat and make a dash for the door, but my boss grabs my arm and pulls me toward the Director of Special Education and tells us both, "You two will shake hands and get back to work on Monday." Against my will I shake the very hand that was on his manhood just moments before! I am shocked into silence and walk out of that building as fast as I can.

The assault is not over yet. Out in the parking lot, my boss follows me outside to my car. The windshield is completely frosted, I get in my car and put the defroster on full blast. I get out of my car to begin the task of scraping frost off my windshield. My boss approaches me and takes the scrapper from my hands, he begins to scrape the windshield and talks as he works. I am standing off to the side clutching my coat to my body tightly because not only do I feel the winter cold, I feel naked, dirty and used by all three of these men, I don't want to talk to him!

Inside my head, I am cursing him out in Spanish! "*Mira cabron sin verguenza, ahora quieres hablar conmigo!*"- "You shameless asshole, now you want to speak to me!" My boss continues scraping my windshield and tells me that he expects me "to get over this by Monday" and that he needs me to continue to work with the Director of Special Education and the entire BOCES staff. He then places the scrapper on the hood of my car and leaves.

My day as a principal is not over yet, I am scheduled to attend a class at Adams State College with the leadership team from my school following this meeting. I drive myself to the college and park my car, the tears are biting at my eyes but there is no time for crying. I am not feeling well as I walk into the building and I need the bathroom. I use a wet paper towel to freshen my face. When I enter the lector hall, I find the teachers from my school already waiting for me inside. They signal a place for me and I join them at the front of the classroom. One of them asked me how things went at the meeting, and I stated, "it did not go well." She just smiled and patted my hand affectionately.

Then the Director of Special Education entered the room and immediately, I wanted to run the hell out of there. I clutched my chair to keep myself from running out the door and I could feel my heart pounding in my chest! I have never reacted to a person's presence as I did in that moment! Once again I was at the scene of the rape and emotionally not present. The instructor began the class once he arrived.

Our team had been invited to this teacher education class to lead a panel discussion on Full Inclusion, the model we had used to return our disabled students to their community school. The instructor turned the meeting over to the Director of Special Education who stood up and began to describe the work that had been accomplished at our school. I could not believe that this man who had professionally raped me within the hour was now praising my leadership and the work of the leadership team. He even became emotional when speaking of how our school had created "the least restrictive environment" for our students! I felt nauseous and sat in silence. I was so thankful for my efficient leadership team because they responded to all the questions and provided clarification of our process.

All I could think of was how I would get out the door and avoid the Director of SPED! I was so preoccupied; I don't remember saying much the entire class. I excused myself from the meeting before my staff and left moments before the class was dismissed. I ran to my car, defrosted the windshield quickly and headed home. As soon as I got in my car alone, I could hear my moans from deep in my stomach which intensified then I was sobbing out loud. I could not stop the flow of tears if I wanted to! I was crying so hard; my vision was blurred. I remember the tissues I had were soaked with tears and snot, I needed more of them and had none. I'm sure the sleeves of my coat became the tissue just so I could clear my eyes and drive.

I remember praying to God to help me get home safely because I was feeling emotions and body pains I had never felt before. I needed his strength and love to get me home tonight. My body was so tense from holding back all emotion since the assault, my muscles were sore. I was gripping the steering wheel so hard, my hands were tingling. I had a hard time controlling the speed of the car because I wanted to get home quickly. I knew the SPED director could also be on the highway since we lived in the same county which only intensified the moment. I was a mess when I got home that evening!

I arrived at home and remembered walking in the door crying and my husband met me with open arms. He asked me what happened, and I just buried my head in his chest and sobbed. He escorted me into our bedroom so our sons would not see me like this. I was thankful they were in their bedrooms playing guitar and did not hear me arrive. In our bedroom, I tried to describe the scenario but all I kept repeating was, "I couldn't stop him!" My response only caused him to ask me, "What did he do to you, tell me." My husband knew the man who had hurt me because they were high school and college classmates. He knew of his violence toward women and had expressed his concern for my working alongside him as a principal. Now I had come home traumatized and I could not describe what had happened at school today. My husband would talk me into taking a shower which brought me back to the present for the moment. I was able to eat the supper he had fixed and reconnect with my sons at the end of the day.

I was so emotionally and physically exhausted at the end of that day but my mind was still racing. I could not stop replaying the act of violence I had experienced earlier at work. I could hear myself saying "stop" and then being drowned out by his hateful and degrading words. I could not get the image of the room out of my head and my being trapped in this room with three very angry men. Only one man delivered the violation for all three of them, while the two white males participated with their silence and inaction. The scene of this professional rape will replay in my mind endlessly because this time I will not be able to pretend nothing happened like I had been able to do with all the other school- based violations. I will never be the same professional woman after this day.

That weekend my make-up consultant came to deliver the items I had ordered and she happened to be a sister-in-law to the Director of SPED. She had called me earlier in the morning to see if I would be home and I really did not want any company. Just hours after the rape, I felt as if my injuries were visible to others, and I did not want anyone to see them or me. These will be the long-term effects of rape I will have to hide in order to function as a principal. I am not ready for what lies ahead.

During our brief conversation, she tells me, "I know what happened on Thursday and I want to talk to you." She would describe how this man had arrived at her home with a six pack of beer and a big smile on his face. He would brag to them, "I fucked her up just as ___ told me to" when retelling the events of the day. He revealed the order came from the Superintendent of Schools. I have left his name blank because his title is more important to me than who he was as a leader. I don't remember anything else she said that day.

I knew at that moment that what happened in that professional meeting was "on purpose" thus intentional and approved by the school board. Superintendents do not take such risks with their credentials unless they have the approval of school board members. I was suddenly flooded with shame and anger which will consume my days. Now I know the SPED director is out bragging about how he had his way with me to others. My life suddenly felt so out of control.

The next Monday, I cannot go to school, instead I make an appointment to see the Superintendent of Schools. I am going to see him because I am not over what happened on November 30,1994 during the professional meeting we both attended! I was shocked by my physical reaction to seeing my boss in person, I immediately started to cry, the tears flowing down my face. It wasn't like me to begin a meeting with the superintendent of schools in tears, but today they ran voluntarily. He looked at me and asked me, "What can I do for you this morning, Gloria?" In between sobs, I answered, "Why didn't you stop him? "I repeated myself before he finally responded, "He's not my employee?" to which I quickly retorted, "But I am!" He did not have a response for me, only the familiar silence I had observed from my boss on Thursday. I will not trust my boss or feel safe in his presence. I cannot look him in the face without crying so I will avoid him in the coming days and weeks. An impossible feat in this small district when he is my immediate supervisor!

Nothing was resolved on November 30th; therefore, I do not know what to expect on a daily basis and what to tell my staff. The leadership team wants to know if the Director of SPED will continue to attend our IEP meetings randomly as he had in the past. I also wonder if he would continue to observe our full inclusion classrooms. As the principal I continue to show up to work only to find myself confined to my office which is so unlike me. I am afraid to venture out to the classroom in case he showed up randomly in a classroom as he used to do. I already knew I would want to run away if I saw him and that would cause a scene at school. Instead, I learned to stay in my office and stare out the small window to the parking lot hoping he would not show up. I hated the way I was acting at school; this was not me! I used to hang out in the classrooms, playground and cafeteria just so I could see the students and support the teachers. I was always ready to do an extra duty or cover a teacher in a classroom. I don't like what is happening to me.

CHAPTER: 17:
"THE DAY THE VEILS CAME DOWN" – GLORIA'S JOURNAL 1994

In 1994, I coined the phrase, "The day the veils came down" to describe the moment when my memory went into overload and no longer had space to store more trauma. I would use this phrase in the book I published in 2017, then I would speak of my unraveling without the knowledge I have today. I had always been able to "pretend nothing happened" in order to continue my career in public education which I loved! After November 30, 1994, I had no room in my memory to file this event. Instead, the memory remained in my consciousness where I relived it day after day while at school. I was never the same professional woman after that day, I was broken, injured and so afraid to talk about what happened during that professional meeting.

Within a week, I found the courage to report the events of November 30th to the only female on the school board. I remember being so anxious while I waited for her to arrive, I was so afraid she would be angry with me for my report. The board member arrived and I was happy to see her. We had always been pleasant and respectful with one another and I felt safe talking to her. As I retold her the events beginning with the IEP meeting when I initially reported the Director of SPED for smelling like alcohol and continuing with the meeting on November 30, 1994, she remained quiet. I remember crying the entire time I was retelling the events which made me look weak in that moment, but I could not stop the voluntary tears. She did not speak for several minutes while I wiped tears from my eyes, blew my nose and took a big sip of water. I was exhausted after reliving the experience in front of a member of the school board who employed me. I waited for a reaction or response from this school official. Finally, she stated calmly and quietly, "This was a professional rape." I was so relieved to hear her validating words and thanked her for her visit. She did not offer any advice, nor did she offer an apology for my experience. When I filed a lawsuit against the school district a year later, she would deny ever visiting my office much less making the comment. The two teachers I defended in the IEP that November morning, would say they "pitied" my reaction to the whole incident in their depositions. They will have to live with their actions as I will.

"The day the veils came down" marks the day I no longer had control over past and present in my life. After this day, my mind would be flooded with all the unresolved school-based traumas dating back to 1962 and I could not make sense out of what was happening to me. Being present in any moment was difficult now, I found myself emotionally absent from the daily functions as principal, wife and mother. I could not make sense of the memories which flooded my consciousness. There was no order or date to these events, they were all mixed up and random, like a box of puzzle pieces without a picture.

For the remainder of the school year, from January to May, I was in a mental battle between past and present which consumed my daily routines. I was not the same educational leader showing up for work any longer. I was unfocused, preoccupied, anxious and sick more days than ever before. I no longer had the capacity to pretend "nothing happened" as I had always done in the past.

I began to mask my emotional and physical pain with any substance I could get my hands on just to be able to continue to report to work. I was now on a continuing contract, so I knew my job was secure for the next school year. However, after November 30th, I no longer had a functional relationship with my boss. I also began to "shut down" and disconnect from my teachers. I was physically sick more often than before and preferred to stay in my office alone when at school. My relationships with the governing board were strained but I continued to fulfill my duties as principal.

When the school year ended, I was physically and emotionally exhausted from trying to pretend my life was normal and "nothing happened". My husband however recognized that what happened to me was a violation of civil rights and knew the timeline for reporting the incident was running out. I had one hundred and eighty days from the date of the incident to report it to the EEOC Equal Employment

Opportunity Council in Colorado. In June of 1995, I reported the incident to the EEOC office and anxiously awaited a response from them.

Next Step: A Mental Health Evaluation and A Medical Scare

Meanwhile, I referred myself to a mental health counselor not far from my home. I was such a mess by the time I asked for help, I was traumatized, angry, depressed, confused, and so lost! I was so thankful the therapist accepted me as her patient. It was hard for her to make sense of my dialogue because I went from past to present in my retelling. I could not talk about just one violation without spilling into other memories. The memory of 1962 surfaced during our sessions, and I could not relate to the content and how it connected to what happened this school year. I was so broken by the vivid memories of first grade which now began to have meaning and purpose in my memories.

I remember leaving her office emotionally spent because I had cried the entire hour of therapy. I will always be grateful to Julie, my therapist in Colorado who taught me to develop "outlets" like dancing, walking, hot baths with Epsom salts and baking soda and writing. During these moments, I took a vacation from trauma, anxiety and depression. I still use these outlets today with the goal of relaxing and being present in my life, a practice I had to relearn.

By July she diagnosed me with PTSD- Post Traumatic Stress Disorder and recommended I see a medical doctor to get a prescription for antidepressants. I had never had a need for such medication in my life and had no idea how it would affect me. I reluctantly made an appointment to see a medical doctor the next week and get a prescription for antidepressants. The female doctor was young and white, she did not spend much time with me, the referral from my therapist made for a short visit. This prescription was for Prozac, and I read all the side effects which should have scared me into not taking any of the pills. I took a pill hoping for some emotional relief and a break from the constant "snowball effect" of unresolved trauma. Within 12 hours my hands were tingling and I began feeling preoccupied about how I was reacting to the medication. I don't remember what happened next, but my husband would tell me, I had had a grand mal seizure right in front of him. He would tell me that I had made a strange comment, then my hands went up and I collapsed on the floor in whole body spasms. When I came to, I was so disoriented I did not recognize him! My body ached from the roots of my hair to the soles of my feet. I could barely walk after a seizure because of the intense pain of my whole body. I could not take care of myself in those moments, and I was so scared of what had just happened to me.

I called and reported the seizure to the doctor who prescribed the medication. She told me to discontinue taking them and to come in for another prescription. This time, I cried a lot with the doctor because I was scared and unsure I wanted to take any more antidepressants despite my emotional health. She had no empathy for my situation, instead she rudely told me, "Gee Gloria, I thought you were a tough cookie!". I left her office in tears and went to fill the second prescription of antidepressants, Zoloft.

My son had an orthodontist appointment the next day and I would have to drive him since my husband was working on the ranch. I was not feeling well when I put my kids in the car and drove to the dentist office. At the dentist office, I became acutely aware of the smells in the office as I sat in the dentist's office with my son. I remember slumping down against the wall because I was about to have another seizure. When I awoke, I was sitting in a dentist chair and my kids were at my side wide eyed and asking me if I was okay. Mom was not okay, my kids called a classmate's mom, and she came to the dentist office to drive us home. I remember the drive home was torture with four kids in the car talking all the way home. After a seizure, all sounds are so magnified you just want to quiet your world.

My husband was very worried about my health now because he could not depend on me to drive myself or the kids anywhere with a seizure condition. The next day, he drove me to the doctor without an appointment. As we sat in the waiting room at the hospital, I did not want to go see the doctor. I wanted to simply stop taking the damn pills and forget about getting relief. The doctor wasn't so critical of me today, probably because my husband had to drive me to the office. Even after my husband described how the anti depressants affect me, I was given another prescription. This time for Wellbutrin. I would have another grand mal seizure at home while vacuuming the living room in our home within 24 hours of taking the medication. My kids were alone with me, and they went running to get a neighbor. When I came to, my husband was explaining to our neighbors that I had been having seizures and that I would be okay. He thanked them for staying with our kids until he got home. I was so disoriented; I didn't recognize the neighbors while they were in my home that day.

CHAPTER 18:
THE BEGINNING OF THE END OF A CAREER IN COLORADO

The first day of school for principals was two weeks away and my emotional health was in critical condition. I was having seizures from medication I had hoped would calm me down and allow me to function at school. I was so afraid of having another seizure in public, which only increased the anxiety I was experiencing. I had not heard back from the EEOC office which meant my employers were not yet informed of the complaint I had submitted in June.

The Leadership Team in our school was organizing a one-day retreat for our staff at a local ranch resort not far from the school. These creative and talented educators put together scavenger hunts and focused sessions to motivate and inspire us as a staff. My presence was altered, and they could see it, I was quiet, preoccupied and unfocused the entire time. I had also lost weight over the summer. I was emotionally disconnected from my educational family, and I did not feel like I belonged with them any longer. I don't remember if I contributed to the educational fun.

The day came when I got the letter from EEOC in Colorado, and they found in my favor. I could now sue the district, the Director of SPED and the Board of Cooperative Services for the violation on November 30, 1994. This governing board represented nine area school districts and I had just made them an enemy by reporting their Director of SPED. So much was at stake, meanwhile my emotional health continued to decline. I discontinued taking the antidepressants but that did not stop the fear of having other seizures while driving or in a meeting with lawyers.

The findings of the EEOC complaint were for Sexual Harassment and I would need to hire an attorney to represent me. Now mind you, I had never had cause or reason to have a lawyer in my life up to now, I was 40 years old. As I began to shop for a lawyer, I found my emotional health a challenge. I could no longer pretend nothing happened even for a few moments; my emotions were so surfaced.

During the first nine weeks of the 1995-1996 school year, my husband would call the district secretary to tell her I would be absent for the day because I could not make the phone call myself. I did not want to go to school because I was sleep deprived, physically sick to my stomach, crying and so preoccupied with the Sexual Harassment lawsuit. The lawyers expected me to stay on the job because it would make for a stronger case against the district. I was scared to death because I could not pretend nothing happened for my husband, my family or the lawyers! I stopped going to work after calling into work sick forty-five days straight.

I was referred to two lawyers from Denver who I hired to represent me in the lawsuit against the school district in the fall of 1995. From the onset, these lawyers had their own agenda for building a successful Sexual Harassment case. They wanted me to be composed, professional, diplomatic, well spoken and remain on the job during the lawsuit. They simply wanted to prove a pattern of behavior for harassing women within this organization. They did not care about the criminal acts these men had imposed on me during a professional meeting! They did not care about my diagnosis or the seizures I had had just weeks prior. With these attorneys I experienced secondary victimization and so much victim shaming!

When my case was tried before a Federal Judge in Denver in a JAG court in January 1996, my PTSD spilled out into the courtroom. I exploded when I heard the Superintendent defend his actions during the November 30, 1994, meeting. He spoke highly of the Director of SPED but not of me! When he stopped speaking, I stood up before the Federal Judge and faced the Superintendent, I said, "I did not go there to get my ass beat up! Why didn't you stop him!" To my left, I could see my lawyers trying to talk me into sitting down and stop talking. My husband was also present and also shocked by my behavior. I was not shocked, the second I heard the Superintendent of Schools speak, I was back in that room being raped again! This time, I wanted a judge to know I had said, "Stop", I was not the weak ass female being portrayed in this courtroom!

The judge would ask him, "why didn't you stop it." The Superintendent of Schools responded with, "I said "time out" to both of them." When the Federal Judge asked me if I wanted to remain in my position as Elementary Principal, I resigned my position on the spot. My lawyers were shocked by my decision! My husband was disappointed and angry because he felt I should have negotiated my return to include paid leave while I recuperated. I no longer respected my boss or any of the board members, how could I fake such a comeback as a PTSD sufferer?

I was now unemployed and about to experience life without family medical insurance for the first time in eighteen years of teaching. I could not see the road ahead for myself at this point. I was masking my pain with alcohol, cigarettes,and pot. Nothing brought me relief! My family would suffer socially and economically as my health declined. I would get a financial settlement from the court and have to sign a disclosure statement following the lawsuit. The financial settlement amounted to "migajas"- bread crumbs in Spanish! The lawyers claimed $30,000 and I was left with the leftovers. I would fire this legal team after one of them made a degrading statement in front of my husband. The lawyer was so frustrated with my behavior in the court and my inability to focus, he finally broke and told me, "Who gives a fuck about the women of the San Luis Valley!"

With the need to hire another lawyer and no income since I resigned my position, I withdrew eighteen years of retirement from my PERA account. I still feel the effects of that financial loss in my life today as a retired person, I don't have enough retirement to live on today. I remember the day I called the representative to ask what my options were given my situation. I agreed to withdraw a monthly stipend to cover our monthly bills knowing the money would run out soon. I would hire a lawyer from a very small firm for a smaller retainer fee, what a mistake!

My emotional health was of no consequence to this lawyer either, his approach was let's go for the "big purse" and make them pay in court. With this lawyer came the need for paralegal work which he did not employ any paralegals in his office. Without giving any thought to my being a PTSD sufferer, he assigned me to interview the women who had reported the workplace violence of the Director of Special Education. I would interview ten professional women who had either worked with him in the same office or worked in other school districts in the area. I had to listen and take notes for the lawyer as each one told me how they had each made him angry in some way at work. Once he was angry at them, each somehow felt obligated to appease his anger by calling him on the phone and apologize. The apology would result in her being lured to a private location where he demanded sex.

An elementary nurse would tell me how she had argued with him during an IEP which made him leave the meeting angry. The following Saturday, she is cleaning house with the music in the background, and finds the Director of Special Education standing in her living room. She reacts by telling him she did not hear his knock and he should not have entered her home. He responded with, "I come to your house to see you and look who's being rude now!" She was too ashamed to give me any more details because he took advantage of the situation. She did not want to testify on my behalf.

Three of the teachers who had filed reports of intimidation and abuse came from the same district that had employed me. They were not shocked by my lawsuit, these three white women had reported him as the Director of Special Education for intimidation, posturing and abusive language. Of the ten women I interviewed, five agreed to testify on my behalf., four white women and one Hispanic female. I realized then that I broke all his rules' when I reported him immediately. I did not try to appease him in any way, instead I reported his workplace violence immediately.

During my second lawsuit, I would be deposed by the defendants legal team representing the larger Special Education agency. My deposition was set for 40 hours in Denver, Colorado which was about four hours by car from home. I would spend more hours being deposed then OJ Simpson who was on trial at the time. This was about breaking me financially and it worked. My husband and I will spend five grueling days in Denver spending money we did not have at the time. The depositions are extremely difficult for me because I have to sit across the table with the man who professionally raped me. However, all the discoveries and evidence fail to mention the rape itself. I felt so misrepresented by attorneys in both lawsuits.

The defense lawyer would ask me if this was the first time, if I had experienced a violation by a school official before and I responded "No". This opened the door for me to talk about the child abuse in 1962. He asked me if I was seeing a counselor and if I had shared this experience with her. I had continued seeing my therapist and she was informed of the childhood trauma I experienced at age six. I was able to state that she had diagnosed me with PTSD. I would become so emotionally charged during these meetings I was sure I would have a seizure from the overload!

In August of 1995 the court found that I could not sue the Director of SPED as an individual and therefore, he was dropped from the case on a legal technicality. The local newspaper used the word "exonerated" to define why he was no longer a defendant in the lawsuit. After that my lawyer began to hint that my case may be thrown out as a result of this finding. He had given up on my case but still wanted to be paid. Within a couple of weeks, the matter was settled out of court, and it was all over for the lawyers. Once again, the lawyer is paid, and I go home without financial stability or resolve. I signed another disclosure statement with this firm which basically stated, "shut up and pretend nothing happened".

CHAPTER 19:
THE WHISTLEBLOWER DANCE

"I danced and sang my way through rage and depression"

Gloria's Journal-1998

When I reported this case to the EEOC, I did not think of myself as a "whistleblower", I am not sure I even understood the meaning of the word. I came to understand the term once I started looking for professional jobs in the area. I was now viewed as a liability to school districts because I had filed a Sexual Harassment lawsuit and no longer marketable as a teacher or principal. At this point in my life, I still do not have a handle on my anxiety, depression, or poor self esteem. I don't even know how to market myself after what I have just experienced. I have now been unemployed for two years and will continue to remain so until something breaks for us.

I find myself alone in my house once our boys go off to school each day. I am still not used to life without teaching or school life after the lawsuit. My husband is working on his father's ranch and managing a property for his Tio Gilbert, so he's gone for hours each day. When I am alone, the past floods me and I feel the anger and anxiety rising inside of me. I also lived in fear of the Director of Special Education stopping by my house unannounced and uninvited. I knew he could walk into my home without knocking because he had done that to other women I had interviewed during the lawsuit. I kept doors locked at all times so often, I would lock my kids out when they were playing outside in the yard! My behavior made no sense to them.

Our boys are now in high school and doing well academically. Despite all the turmoil in our lives, our family will find a positive outlet in music! We bought our sons electric guitars when they expressed an interest in learning to play music in junior high. Neither of them were interested in playing high school sports in this school district. So, we supported their interest in learning to play an instrument knowing the discipline it would take for them to play the music of their choice. Our oldest son played bass guitar and our youngest son played lead guitar. Our sons brought music into our home daily. Hearing, listening or playing music became an outlet to our circumstances, we enjoyed together as a family. Our boys would perform their Heavy Metal riffs and play along with their favorite artists, Metallica, Pantera, Nirvana, Green Day and a lot of the classic rock I grew up with myself.

I started listening to Spanish music when they were practicing in their rooms. I am very grounded in Spanish music having grown up in a home where I saw my parents dance to these rhythms. My husband and I were former dancers as undergraduate at ASC college's *Semillas de la Tierra*, Ballet Folklorico dance troop. Therefore we still loved to go out dancing to New Mexico, Texas and Mexican music.!

 I will spend hours dancing my way through rage and depression in the privacy of my bedroom. I bathed myself in the Spanish language while I danced which brought me great joy and relieved my body pain. I loved the cumbia rhythms of *Selena y Los Dinos* and learned to sing three of her songs. The words of their songs brought relief to me because they expressed the pain of losing something or someone you love. The song "*Como La Flor*" was about being betrayed by someone you love and having to separate yourself from the toxic relationship. The song " *Las Cadenas*" was a song about setting boundaries for yourself in a relationship and knowing when to leave. *"No debes jugar con mi carino" w*as a song about setting boundaries and confronting abuse in a relationship. The words resonated with me because I was in love with something that did not love me back, my career in public education.

I could not find words in English to express what I felt inside like I did in Spanish. I had spent a lot of money on Self Help books about depression, trauma and abuse only to find the content unrelatable to my trauma. There were few if any self help books to deal with the abuse of school officials. Furthermore, I did not find English words healing like the words in Spanish. The English language had been weaponized in too many of my school experiences and I found little comfort in this language at this point in my life.

Then, in February 1996, my husband who had been the pillar holding our family together, had an acute pancreatitis. He would spend eleven days in the hospital during which time he was diagnosed with type 2 diabetes. My husband had experienced and lived the stress of my career all those years. He had been with me every step of the way even when he did not agree with me. Tomas loved me when I did not recognize the woman in the mirror myself. Now he was seriously sick, and his life would change forever. He was prone to diabetes because it ran in his family but it was our lifestyle and stress that put on the weight which resulted in his onset of diabetes. The hospital bill was enormous, and we did not have health insurance. Suddenly, I had to pull myself together and go find a job immediately.

He's Back in my Life….

I would get a job as a Head Start director in the fall of 1997 of a local center. The financial relief was welcomed, and we seemed to be moving in a positive direction. Then, **he** was back in my life, the man I had reported and taken to federal court was back in my life as a member of the Head Start governing board. He had been visiting the facility at all hours of the day when board members were on site. He made sure I knew he was around though he never spoke to me. I had heard hints that he wanted to get on the board since one board member was resigning within a month.

The next Head Start meeting was held at the center site furthest from home. I had caught a carpool to the meeting with board members that evening. I did not ask to see the agenda before the meeting and no one spoke about it on the way. Imagine my surprise when he came walking into the Head Start meeting that evening to be officially sworn in as a board member. I refused to work for the man whose violence I had taken to court in my last professional position. I was so angry with the board members because they knew about my lawsuit and the fact that I had reported his violence. I remember stating to the board that evening, "I will not work for this man, you cannot expect me to" as I walked out of the meeting.

I would be "fired" at the next governing board meeting for insubordination with the man present and once again enjoying the power he had over my life. My sons witnessed my firing because I was too afraid to show up by myself. I knew then our family would have to leave the area to begin again. This man would not allow my family to remain in the area without his constant interference in our lives. From the lawsuit I had learned he had clout with his family, politicians, government officials and law enforcement. That very evening, I went to the Sheriff's office in our county to file a report. My report detailed the "stalking behavior" this male demonstrated prior to his becoming my boss this very evening. I was laughed at by the deputies on duty when I requested a copy of the report. One of them commented to me, "You let him get to you!" I was not allowed a copy of the report therefore I have no evidence of having filed a report in the sheriff's office.

CHAPTER 20:
MY LAST DAYS IN COLORADO

Once again, I was unemployed in an area of the state where I had no credibility as a professional female. Once our oldest son graduated high school in 2000 and our youngest son was a sophomore in high school, we discussed the idea of selling our home and moving out of the area. As a family, we recognized the need to relocate and start over in a new location. This meant our youngest son would be uprooted in the middle of his high school experience. He would choose to stay behind and live with a family friend instead of leaving his high school. I would be so thankful when he rejoined us at our new setting at the end of the first grading period and even more thankful when the transition was positive for him. His ability to play guitar was the perfect "icebreaker" when he arrived at his new high school. We had accumulated a lot of debt remaining in this area and only faced more unemployment if we had stayed. It would mean leaving our aging parents who lived within thirty minutes of our home. We had always planned on living near them to help with end-of-life activities. Now, we were about to put a lot of distance between us.

That summer, I would be recruited to apply for an intermediate principal position in another *Colorado* public school. Though I was unemployed at the time, my professional network was still active. On his visit to the area, a superintendent and his wife came to visit me personally and invite me to apply for the vacancy in his district. Chuck knew about the lawsuit I had filed but he also knew I had been effective in my first principal position. He told me, "You deserve a second chance and I know your determination, Gloria." He took a chance on me and hired me to run a 4th through 6th grade elementary school. I was hopeful once again that perhaps my career could rebound elsewhere in this state.

However, without mental health therapy, my leadership now included PTSD. The biggest challenge I faced in returning was that I did not feel safe in schools any longer. I did not trust my employers, the school board members, nor did I want to be part of their social network.

Over the next three years, I called in sick a lot because I felt safer at home. The superintendent who hired me would be fired at the end of the school year and I would survive in this district for another two years. I knew the work of a principal and how to supervise and work alongside teachers, I knew how to respond to the demanding paperwork and how to comply with the daily operations of the school.

However, I did not feel connected to the teachers or my work in this school because I used so much energy trying to hide from my past and my symptoms which were getting harder to hide. At the time, my husband and I were volunteering our time to coach a local community dance team who were without a teacher at the time. With the approval of the superintendent who hired me, I continued to share my knowledge of Mexican folklore dances with this student group on weekends. Their performance schedule kept us busy on weekends performing in the area. The members of this dance team were students in the district from elementary through high school. I loved the cultural fill I experienced in each practice; I loved being bathed in the rhythms of Spanish music. Once again, I had found a reason to dance and be joyful! It was the outlet I needed to keep my sanity and ignore my trauma.

Then, the high school principal became the superintendent and within six months, he placed me on administrative leave with pay. The man did not like me as a colleague and much less as a member of his leadership team. On his first day as superintendent, he let me know if I got on his bad side, he would fire me. True to his word he got rid of me by the beginning of the second semester. As this job assignment ended, I felt I was living a DeJa'Vu moment because there were so many similarities and triggers to my previous experience in this administrative assignment.

At this time, I felt as if my career had hit rock bottom in Colorado and I would need to leave the state to restart my career in public education. I began to look at job openings in New Mexico which piqued my interest immediately. Most of the teaching job openings in northern New Mexico school districts preferred bilingual candidates! With my credentials I knew I would be marketable in this area of the state! I continued to watch for openings and applied for licensure with their bureau. I learned about the reciprocity agreement between Colorado and New Mexico which enabled me to get licensed within 90 days. Once I had signed a teaching contract, my husband and I relocated to the area where I would be teaching that fall.

CHAPTER 21:
MY 1962 CLASS REUNION: I HAD TO KNOW.

Before I left Colorado, I vowed to make contact with the first-grade classmates who had made the trip to the Teacher's house in 1962. I have been able to recognize the faces and names of my classmates after relieving these memories many times since 1995. I was shocked by one of my classmates because we had ridden the school bus together for twelve years, we were neighbors, our families knew each other, and she had been my sister-in-law for thirteen years! We were connected in so many ways, yet we had never spoken about what we did at the Teacher's house when we were six years old.

Now, here I am, knocking at her door and hoping she remembers something. For me, it's a moment I have dreaded because I had to know if the memories were real or if I was having a mental breakdown! We hugged and greeted each other, and she invited me into her house. Amada (not her real name) and I had not seen each other in the past few years. I had a hard time getting to the point because all I had were pieces of memories from first grade, and I didn't know how to even start the conversation. I was very emotional at that moment cause it was as if we were both six years old again and talking like we used to as children. I asked her if she remembered going to the teacher's house with me. She responded, "Yes, I remember". Once she said yes, I was ready with a lot of questions.

Why did the teacher take us to her house? She said I would come to her desk to talk to her, and we both got in trouble. She told me, "That is why I never talked in school again."

What did we do when we got to the teacher's house? She remembered the "weenie dogs" and all the shit we cleaned up on the floor. She remembered being nauseated by the smell of dog shit and the places we had to crawl to find it.

Why did we get in trouble? We got in trouble because we talked Spanish to each other, and the teacher would hear us. Once she heard us, we would be taken to her house after lunch. She helped me understand that these visits happened frequently after we ate lunch in the cafeteria.

About two weeks later, I traveled fifty miles to meet up with Diego (not his real name), the six-year-old boy who went with us to the Teacher's house. I had figured out his last name and associated it with a family restaurant in the area. I showed up at the restaurant hoping to make contact with him and ended up finding him at the restaurant that day. We sat down in a booth, and I began to tell him about my memories of first grade and how he was involved. I was surprised by his response, "That teacher hated Mexicans. She hated us." His tone was angry, and he was annoyed by my questions because he could not understand how I did not remember what had happened until then. I did not know how to explain that to him because I did not understand myself. Diego remembered the dogs and the clean-up duty we performed, but he did not want to discuss the details. "It's disgusting to know what she made us do. I hated school after that!"

I would learn that Diego did not graduate from high school and realize his birthright in this country. He had only attended first grade with me, and then he had moved out of the area. Amada never spoke in any classes I had with her thereafter. She was a salient student. She did not raise her hand to participate in class discussions, and now I understand why she did not want to show her brilliance as a student after age six.

After visiting with my classmates the summer before I left *Colorado*, I felt better about myself because they had validated the memories that had haunted me for some time. Amada and I continue to communicate and enjoy each other's company to this day. She baptized our oldest son which only strengthened the bond between us. Our children were inseparable once they began to enjoy music and playing guitar together. They often entertained our families with their skillful guitar playing. Amada and I are both bilingual speakers who enjoy conversations in two languages at all times. Our first-grade experiences still surface in our conversations as adults. She remembered the butterfly earrings we made for Mother's Day and the days we had to stay in for recess to finish our presents. I am so thankful to have her in my life now that we both know what happened in first grade 1962.

"A Mind is a Terrible Thing to Waste"- A Civil Rights Quote I recall as I think about the oppression we experienced at age six.

CHAPTER 22:
RESTARTING MY CAREER AT AGE 48

"My goal in New Mexico was to complete my career goal, instead I confronted my past and found a place to heal and belong"
- Gloria Elena Lopez-2023

I left Colorado with the hope of restarting and returning to my career in bilingual education. I also left without seeking professional counseling for my PTSD which was like a shadow in my life, always there to remind me of the past. I was more afraid of the stigma of having a psychological injury and the need for therapy that I avoided and ignored my own symptoms until I could not any longer. Tomas was able to get a job in his professional field within six months and we settled down in our new surroundings. Neither one of us had lived outside of Colorado before and we had a hard time acclimating to the desert heat the first year, but we loved the mild winters immediately!

In New Mexico I was motivated and encouraged by the fact that I had the opportunity to run schools with bilingual programs. I was confident about my abilities to present instruction in two languages and felt I could find a place for my skill set in New Mexico. I had a false sense of well being as I began my career in New Mexico. I had no idea how or when the "triggers and doubt" would restart as I began to spend time in schools and classrooms. I was hired to teach at an elementary school with a bilingual program and I accepted the position to teach the 2004-2005 school year in New Mexico.

When I moved to New Mexico, I made the sacrifice to restart my career knowing I could never talk to a future employer about my emotional health because I risked becoming a liability in any district. I decided to keep this secret for another fourteen years so I could finish the professional goal I set for myself at age twenty. I had left Colorado with three years of retirement, so I basically restarted my career at ground zero at the age of forty-eight.

Teaching in New Mexico meant I would teach in the only state in our nation with bilingual education in their constitution. Each school district who applied for the bilingual program would get state funding to support their programs. These funds were used for teacher salaries and program materials within each district's general fund. The schools then hired teachers with endorsements in bilingual education and TESOL- Teaching English as a Second Language to comply with the state requirements. Each school district selected the bilingual program model for its schools which provided one or more hours of Spanish Language arts and one hour of ESL instruction for those students who qualified for these services.

My credentials from Colorado qualified me for a TESOL endorsement, without having to take additional classes to earn the endorsement. I would have to take *La Prueba,* a Spanish language test which tested my ability to speak, read, write and listen in the language. I took the test twice because I forgot to turn on my microphone during the first test and did not record a mock parent conference. After I earned my endorsements in bilingual education, I felt a pride in myself I had not felt in years, I felt free to speak Spanish in school once again!

However, the conditions imposed by federal and state guideline for program implementation schools will be the sole trigger to my child abuse at age six. This trigger will challenge my ability to perform as a teacher or principal until I retire in 2017.

Linguistic Segregation: The trigger that I could not silence.

At the age of six I collided with linguistic segregation on the first day of school when I entered a world where the languages I spoke were now separate and unequal in value. When the English language was used by my first-grade teacher to devalue and degrade the knowledge I brought to the classroom as a Spanish speaker, her efforts were not about teaching me to speak English or instructing me in English, it was about imposing an inferiority for the knowledge and voice I possessed in

Spanish. Though I am Caucasian by race, I have never felt white enough in public schools because I am bilingual and bicultural. In my own educational journey, linguistic segregation was rationalized as 'full immersion education" which meant there was no language mixing in these classrooms, it was always speak English or else. If one immerses a Spanish speaker long enough with English only instruction, it drowns the language and many will believe it is gone forever in their lives. They no longer think, read, speak or write in Spanish. Their Spanish voices are silent.

In New Mexico, I will collide and be triggered to my elementary trauma by the presence of linguistic segregation in every school I am assigned to over the next fourteen years. For me, linguistic segregation continues to be the "white elephant in the room" which I cannot ignore or get around, it's always present at school. In my professional development classes and English language conferences, this approach to instruction was also referred to as the "foreign language model", which assumes that students have little or no experience with the target language. However, I found that only a minority of students in New Mexico are actually foreign language speakers learning English for the first time in our lives. The rest of the student population are dominant English speakers who were born and raised in New Mexico. These Spanish surnamed students have been English speakers for five or more generations and today are limited Spanish speakers.

Yet, the end of year high stakes school data from English tests in reading, math and science continues to be evidence and proof of our poor performance in English. As a subgroup in this country, Hispanics, which includes all Spanish surnamed students in the nation, continue to lag behind their English speaking counterparts on standardized tests since 1969 when the first Iowa test of Basic skills was administered. I was in junior high and remember the stress of taking the test alongside my peers in a cafeteria. The data results have remained the same for Hispanics, Blacks and Native American students who account for the achievement gap in public education after all these decades of English only education.

For the next fourteen years, I will watch and witness the effects of linguistic segregation on the lives of my students in New Mexico. The full immersion model is contrary and unnatural to the way English, Spanish and Tribal cultures coexist in Colorado and New Mexico. Culture and language are not separated in the lives of these students, like my own upbringing, these languages are spoken simultaneously in their homes, stores and communities.

In my own family, we did not speak English in the morning and Spanish in the afternoon, we spoke both languages simultaneously. These language patterns of mixing languages in speech also existed in the lives of my students in New Mexico. There were no rules or conditions about when these languages or their value, they co-existed just like the people they represented. I hate the stereotypes that are often associated with these speaking patterns, that we speak "Spanglish" or that we are "mochos" and do not speak either language appropriately. The lowest of expectations was hearing English reading specialists define ESL students and teachers as weak in two languages, therefore you eliminate the unnecessary language to ensure proficiency in the dominant language.

It takes intelligence and HOT, Higher Order Thinking skills to express yourself in two languages and an even higher order skill to speak each language according to its language patterns and rules. It is not a skill a monolingual English speaking teacher can provide students in this country and yet they are the majority among licensed teachers in this country.

American public schools in the southwest still segregate English and Spanish during instruction. Our Spanish surnamed families feared ethnic segregation in this country in the early 1900's because their Spanish speaking children could be denied access to schools with white monolingual English speaking children. I recall one such lawsuit in Alamosa, Colorado in 1913 where a family sued the state and won its case against racial segregation. The only school these students attended until this lawsuit was called "The Mexican School" which provided bilingual instruction to its students. After this, these same students will experience English only education and be shamed for their Spanish knowledge in many ways.

However, linguistic segregation has been just as lethal to Spanish surnamed people and their communities. Today many US Spanish speakers no longer speak Spanish and prefer to only always speak English after twelve years of public education. The full immersion, English only system has created a monolingual English-speaking society of today which has all but silenced the Spanish and Tribal voices of the southwest United States.

As American citizens, Spanish surnamed citizens have been led to believe that we will be more accepted as Americans IF we gave up our Spanish voices and the brilliance of the language. This notion has brainwashed many southwest citizens, Spanish surnamed and Tribal, into abandoning their heritage languages and speak only in English. However, my life experience has taught me that speaking English in the United States does not change your DNA, your family history or your last name. Neither does it not make you more acceptable in American culture. The self denial of culture and language takes a toll on our psyche over time.

As a PTSD sufferer, I was "triggered" by the second-class status of the Spanish language in New Mexico. When full immersion education is present, English will be the language of instruction and Spanish will be the other language but not a valued academic language. The most obvious trigger to me was the fact that in schools with a two-hour bilingual program, students receive five hours of English only instruction and one hour of Spanish only instruction. In a Dual Language school where I taught, the model was 50-50. Students would spend half of their day in English-only instruction and the other half in Spanish-only instruction. However, Dual language schools still take national standardized tests which only value gains made in the English language. In my opinion, this is the definition of ethnic segregation, separate and unequal treatment of students at school based on their heritage language.

To this day, students who come to school speaking Spanish are immediately labeled, ESL-English as a Second Language or ELD-

English Language Development because their families admit to speaking Spanish in the home on the home language survey they complete when registering their children in any school in the United States. Over time, many Spanish speaking parents simply deny their heritage language and claim to only speak English just to avoid the labels and stereotyping of public schools. When I reflect on my own experience, I know my parents would have proudly claimed they spoke English and Spanish at home. My parents loved their English and Spanish voices all their lives and would never have denied their knowledge in Spanish. Why should any Spanish-surnamed parent have to deny their brilliance in this world language?

Once these Spanish speaking students are labeled ESL or ELD, they become a "problem" to classroom teachers who are pressured to increase and improve their class data by the end of the school year. ESL students historically have low test scores on English standardized tests. ESL students are divided up and assigned to those classrooms with ESL-endorsed teachers. TESOL teachers receive a stipend of $1500 dollars for each school year. Each district sets data goals in English at the beginning of the school year and will monitor the progress of students throughout the year. The biggest problem ESL students face in classrooms is that most of their teachers do not speak Spanish and those that do pretend they no longer speak the language. Instead, the burden falls on the student to accommodate the teacher. The student is left to figure out the content and language rules with a teacher who can only deliver instruction one language at a time.

The long-term effects of linguistic segregation played out in my classrooms in New Mexico. As a classroom teacher, my teaching schedule called for me to teach five hours of English instruction and forty five minutes of Spanish Language arts daily. The students in my class spoke two dialects of Spanish, I had students who spoke Mexican Spanish and I had a larger population of USA Spanish speakers. I also had Tewa students who attended their own isolated forty-five-minute class in their heritage language.

The students who spoke Mexican Spanish were labeled ESL, and required more testing in English than their peers. These students often scored at beginning to nearing proficient in English. The students who spoke USA Spanish and Tewa were often labeled ELD- needing English Language Development, they scored between nearing proficient to proficient on standardized English tests, but few scored advanced. Each teacher was also required to provide an additional forty five minutes of daily academic interventions in English to their students scoring below proficient. I referred to this insane strategy as "magic English lessons" because teachers were to invent, create or design strategies in English beyond those they had already tried with this student population. The practice is truly the definition of insanity, "to do the same thing over and over again and expect a different result".

During English language instruction, I would monitor the progress of my elementary students on a weekly basis. I was teaching second grade at the time, and I remember testing one student group seventeen times in a grading period only to get the same results. The student would make gains one week and losses the next. I was having to comply with this punishing test schedule which kept my students from recess or PE to keep in the good graces of English language data specialists who were so attached and guarded about the damn data! In my opinion, these data specialists spend their time berating classroom teachers who have no "magic" left in their English lessons!

As a district, I remember the celebrations and elations expressed by school officials when one school made significant gains in their English data in either English Language arts, Math or Science. That principal and school would then be the model for the rest of the schools to reach their data goals of making five to ten percent gains in a grading period of forty-five days. As a bilingual educator,I could not relate to their celebrations and joy of contributing to a monolingual English society in New Mexico.

I hated sitting through data meetings on a monthly basis because I would have to present my student data in front of my peers. I could certainly never do enough in English to close the data gap for students in my classroom. Meanwhile I am teaching one to two hours of Spanish which has NO academic value and is not part of the data formula. I remember the day I stood up in a data meeting as a principal and dared to challenge their findings from a bilingual perspective by stating that when I looked at the data, I saw the presence of two or more languages, English,Spanish and Tewa and not the "achievement gap" in English they seemed to dwell on continually. I was simply dismissed after my statement and the next principal continued with their failing English data which garnished more attention from this group of educators. How could this group of school officials have so much faith in this English language data which ignored and denied the ethnic brilliance of their students and themselves?

I remember one principal calling me into the office to voice their disappointment in my student data. This Hispanic female administrator accused me of not providing sufficient English interventions to my ESL students and threatened to put me on a "teacher improvement plan" if my data did not improve by the end of the year. Meanwhile this principal had me teaching two hours of Spanish so she could get the maximum amount allotted by the bilingual program for her school. She was lacking a Spanish language teacher and had assigned me to teach an additional hour of Spanish. I was not providing English interventions to my students; I was accommodating the lack of Spanish language teachers.

I was being punished for not making enough data gains in English and being neglectful of my student needs. I was triggered by my own painful past as a Spanish speaker. All I could think of was leaving this position and finding another home for my skills as I had always done when hate and evil showed its face. My attendance as a teacher tanked during these times. I made up any excuse to stay home where I felt safe. I did not feel safe at school knowing I had to answer to a principal who I no longer respected.

I found many Hispanic female administrator's unwilling to speak Spanish even though they employed a significant Spanish speaking staff. I was shocked by their "stop signs" when I spoke Spanish in front of them. They would raise one hand to signal, "I don't speak Spanish" and many would raise two hands to signal, "stop speaking Spanish" to me immediately. I was too familiar with this same behavior from white male administrators and teachers in *Colorado* who demanded these same accommodations from students and myself because they only spoke English. In New Mexico, I found the same demand for accommodations from several Hispanic female administrators who behaved as if they had never spoken or heard a word of Spanish living in New Mexico. This is a state where 63% of the state's counties are named in Spanish or Tewa languages, not to mention the rivers, streets and towns. It also has the best Mexican food with menus written in Spanish. I could not relate to their disrespect for the heritage languages of their students and their own.

I remember the day that as an elementary principal I went to turn in the State Bilingual applications for the school I was running at the time. I walked into the office of the Director of Instruction with the ESL - English as a Second Language portion of the application. She was Hispanic and I began talking in English and Spanish about the process. Then without any reservations, she looked at me and stated, "Gloria, you have a bad habit of speaking Spanish whenever you want, let's stop that." I simply handed over the application for my building and answered the rest of her questions in English only. I felt so stupid and ashamed for her comment, but she felt so empowered by her posture behind the desk. It's one thing to be dumbed down by white males in *Colorado* but to have this experience in New Mexico from females, was unacceptable to me. I did not thrive in their presence or grow in these environments and neither did many of my students.

Between 2010 and 2012, my parents were in and out of hospitals continually until their death two months apart in the fall of 2012. At the age of 89 my mother was diagnosed with colon cancer in 2010 and as a principal, I took a twelve-week medical leave without pay to sit by her side in a Denver hospital. This was frowned upon by several Hispanic central administrators who imposed unnecessary guilt on me when they would have put their families first given the situation. I remember the day the assistant superintendent called me to her office to question my absences. I was still expected to complete my end of year evaluations and make hiring decisions while on leave and made several trips from Denver to New Mexico during this time to make this happen. This Hispanic female administrator made me call the hospital where my mother was a patient to verify my absence. I was so ashamed when I had to call my moms doctor and have him verify that I was indeed at the hospital with my mom. The doctor actually told me I needed to find a healthier place to teach but I got this intolerant Hispanic educator off my back for the moment.

The Unraveling at the End of My Career

I was right to not trust school officials with my painful past, it was hard to survive one school year at a time in New Mexico. In 2013 I left this district and accepted a position as a bilingual resource teacher in the community I lived in. It was also the birthplace of my paternal grandfather. I was once again hopeful that I would be valued in this position instead, it would once again be a test of my ability to tolerate full immersion education. I would be providing Spanish language arts to an intermediate school with fourth and fifth grade students.

The Hispanic principal of the school did not speak a word of Spanish and made it known during our interview. She was very positive about my joining her team of teachers and was pleased with my education and background as a Spanish Language arts teacher. I was so excited about the possibilities for success at this school and so happy I would only be teaching Spanish all day long! I would have six classes of Spanish with two double sized classes the first two years I taught in this district. I found myself teaching Spanish to over 200 students per day in a gymnasium with horrible acoustics. I had a classroom which could only sit twenty-five students at a time, so the gym was used to teach double size classes. I had to use a microphone to be heard over the furnace blowers and the dominant English speakers who talked right over me in this setting. I had permission to begin a dance program at this school which would be therapeutic for me and so much fun for my students!

I loved being in class and looking at the sea of faces before me that looked just like me! My students were for the most part Spanish surnamed, brown skinned and proud of their community! I was expected to use the district approved Spanish language arts program which I had used in the previous district. This program was meant to be a full immersion Spanish Language arts program and I was expected to deliver instruction using 80% Spanish and 20% English with minimal translations. The students in my classes spoke two dialects, Mexican Spanish and USA Spanish. In my classroom that meant the Mexican students grasped the concepts in Spanish more readily than the US

Spanish speakers who were limited in their ability to speak and express themselves in Spanish. I recognized that for my Mexican students, this was the only time during their school day when they were "smarter and more vocal " than the US Spanish speakers and they were vocal in my classes. For my US Spanish speakers, they struggled to express themselves and could not function in the Spanish LA materials provided by the district. I could not challenge the Mexican Spanish speakers without leaving the US Spanish speakers struggling and silent in my classes. This did not foster respect between these student groups which will play out in high school culture when they segregate as Mexicans and US Spanish speakers.

I remember the day I had a small group of USA Spanish speakers in my classroom who were limited Spanish speakers and I asked them privately," Why don't you want to speak Spanish with me in class?" I was shocked when a fifth-grade girl responded with, "Ms. Lopez, we don't want to look Mexican!" I was shocked by her response and yet it made complete sense given my history. My own first grade teacher had told me, "Stop speaking Mexican!" implying that speaking Spanish was a function of Mexican people. I found myself explaining to the group that speaking only in English does not change our connection to this language because of our last names, family pictures and our ties to Mexico. I felt powerless to change the fact that my students were learning to deny their heritage and abilities to speak this world language.

"Our language is the reflection of ourselves"
Cesar Chavez

As a bilingual resource teacher, I dedicated one day of the week to dancing and singing in the gym because I wanted to give my students an authentic experience in language and culture. I wanted them to feel good in the skin they wore and their Spanish surnames. As a former dancer and performer, I choreographed traditional Mexican dance and American line dances to engage and entertain my students. Each class started with *"La Marcha de La Gente"*- "The March of the People" which is a group dance performed at weddings but I put a Social Studies twist on it and used it to teach the elements of community. I taught them to sing the traditional Spanish birthday song, *"Las Mananitas"* with seven verses all about you and the day you were born. I used YouTube videos to help them understand the meaning of this complicated song. In this song we are born Saints who are celebrated by the heavens, family and nature. They also learned to sing the New Mexico state song in Spanish, *"Así es Nuevo México"* and met *Roberto Mondragon,* the New Mexico artist who recorded the song. I loved singing with my students on Fridays because it was the only time I could actually engage them in their beautiful Spanish voices as a whole class.

During dance class, we danced to New Mexico Spanish music, Mexican folk dances and popular line dances at the time. I loved dancing because I knew the therapeutic value as an outlet to my own unresolved trauma. The fun and challenge came in teaching them the intricate steps with large student groups. I was thankful the teachers came to class with them and were willing to help manage them while I was teaching. We danced to the music of Sparx, a popular and gifted group of female singers who happen to be sisters and reside in New Mexico! *"El de Los Ojos Negros"*- "The One with the Dark Eyes", became a popular cumbia rhythm we danced in a circle and with several classes, it was awesome to see four large *cumbia* circles dancing this to this beautiful New Mexico rhythm.

During the month of May, I was expected to put on an end of year Cultural Celebration showcasing what students learned in class. It was amazing to watch these beautiful students perform and dance in their heritage languages with so much pride and purpose to their actions. The Tewa students performed traditional tribal dances and presented themselves in their traditional names. The Spanish language students performed dances to traditional and New Mexico music. They used their Spanish voices loudly as they sang *"Las Mananitas" and "Así es Nuevo México"* for their families. For sixty minutes this school community is bathed and immersed in the heritage languages of their people by their children. What feels so natural on this evening of celebration gives way to a school culture that reflects an English only society.

Then in 2016, the presidential race ignited the "Me Too Movement" in our country and I was thrown back into the unresolved trauma from the Sexual Harassment case I had filed in 1995 in Colorado. The more I listened to the many professional women coming forward with their own stories related to sexual abuse and harassment in the workplace, the more vibrant and intrusive my own memories became. I felt so out of control emotionally at the beginning of the 2017-2018 school year and unsure about how to proceed.

I decided I would take the risk of letting a school official know about my health concern, what a mistake! I made an appointment to see the superintendent of schools to inform him of my health concern. I became emotional and confused in my delivery of what I was experiencing. The only thing he heard was that I was dissatisfied with my room assignment and being the bilingual resource teacher in his district. In the end I was shocked into silence once again by a superintendent who simply told me, "Gloria, teaching Spanish is about the money, you should know that."

After that I did not hear anything else he said, I felt like he took an eraser and erased my purpose in this school district. He lost me as his employee with that comment and so when he came to see me on the day I retired, December 7, 2017, he could not reel me back in despite his efforts. I told him, "I'm unraveling and I can't stop it."

I told myself I had accomplished my career goal of retiring from public education after fourteen years of service in New Mexico. I was able to retire on the 75 rule which states that if your age and years of service equal 75, you can retire. On December 7, 2017, I officially retired from public education at the age of 62 plus fourteen years of service.

CHAPTER 23:
THE HEALING POWERS OF NUEVO MEXICO

In New Mexico, I find solace and healing in the rich cultures of the state. I am able to listen to Spanish music with bilingual programming on several radio stations. One minute you are listening to a fabulous *corrido* and then the animated radio host greets you in English with the name of the artist and the song. Everyday is a birthday celebration for somebody and you hear the radio host say, "Today, we have many birthdays to celebrate, this special *'Feliz Cumpleanos* goes out to so and so from your *familia and your Madrina* and your *primos* who love you very much*!* The next song is a rendition of the "*Las Mananitas'*' by a variety of artists from the USA and Mexico.

This is how language occurs naturally in my life and in the lives of many New Mexican citizens. I love being able to listen and dance to New Mexico artists performing live in local casinos, "*Al Hurricane Sr. and Jr.", Los Blue Ventures," "Lorenzo Antonio," " Sparx,", "Ernestine Romero", "Perfeccion," and "Darren Cordova y Calor",* are a few of the great bands I have danced to while living in the area. Their abilities to speak both languages are often included in their music when they provide Spanish renditions to English songs, like "The Wild Side of Life " by Lorenzo Antonio and his sisters Sparx. I love the language diversity of the people in the stores and streets because English, Spanish and Tewa are so common everywhere I go in this state. This is the America my students live in as well. At a personal level, these are the healing elements I found living among the people of New Mexico and I am grateful to them. Since moving to New Mexico, I have had access to all these languages which define who I am as a citizen and in my world one language is not more valuable than another or segregated.

I am Mestiza, more Indian than European who grew up speaking Spanish and English in the southwest United States. Today, English and Spanish are world languages and I have had the ability to speak both all my life. I do not need a passport to discover my roots or family history. The furthest south I can trace my family history in the USA is northern New Mexico where I now reside. I live where I came from, this is my Mexico and my United States of America. I have no lineage in Mexico or any other Spanish speaking country. My blood history tells the story of a person who lives where they came from, I have no immigrant story of my family arriving here from someplace else.

On July 4th, 1776, while the USA was celebrating its independence from Great Britain, my ancestors were living in the 30 percent of this country that was still Mexico. Mexico then and now was occupied by tribal communities, many who learned to speak Spanish in order to survive the displacement which came with the colonization by the Spaniards in the early 1500's and continued for 300 years. The catholic church furthered this effort with Spanish speaking priests who befriended them and taught them catholicism. The conquistador took without asking from area tribal communities and rationalized the practice with a sword in one hand and a cross in the other. The Spanish language was often used to oppress and control the Indians who did not speak the language or understand the culture of the Spaniard. Overtime, the Spanish government claimed lands that were occupied by tribal people without permission or respect for the people. These practices by the Spanish government allowed them to colonize and claim the lands and their natural resources for mother Spain. These experiences will be repeated in their lives after 1848 with a new government and new language, English.

Meanwhile Spanish men married or claimed Indian women as their wives and their offspring learned to speak Spanish and their tribal language. The mixing of Spanish and Indian bloodlines surfaces in our blood history across the southwest. Until I submitted a sample of my blood to learn my blood history, I would have told you I grew up in a home which identified themselves as Spanish Americans only and not of Mexican descent. As a college student, I took my first Mexican American history class and learned that we were more Mexican than Spanish because of our indigenous bloodlines. Overtime, I have accepted and learned to love my own history and diversity as a Mexican American citizen.

I found this poem in an elementary bilingual reading comprehension series, and I shared it with my students in New Mexico. This poem describes the bilingual experience in America through a student's eyes. He describes the pride he feels in speaking English and Spanish and the linguistic intelligence that he will acquire over time. I share the same desire with this student for these two languages to be joined in a river of knowledge where everyone who speaks these languages can drink this rich water without fear.

After all, we live in the world's largest English-speaking country, and we live in the world's second-largest Spanish-speaking country in the world.

Between Two Languages
by Juan Manuel García

I'm proud that I can speak both English and Spanish.
But I feel like jelly in a sandwich
or a river between two mountains.
I feel my head is filled with words.
It makes me feel smart.
I know I can get a job
because I speak two languages.
I can help clients who speak Spanish,
and since I know English,
I can help my dad.
I like to translate for my dad
and teach English to my little brother and sister.
I'm proud of my two languages,
but sometimes I feel as if
the Spanish speakers are on one mountain,
the English speakers on the other,
and I wish I could push them into the river
so we could all be together.

Entre dos idiomas
por Juan Manuel García

Yo estoy orgulloso de que puedo hablar inglés y español.
Pero me siento como mermelada en un sandwich
o como un río entre dos montañas.
Siento que mi cabeza está llena de palabras.
Me hace sentir inteligente.
Sé que puedo encontrar trabajo
porque hablo dos idiomas.
Puedo ayudar a clientes que hablan español
y, porque hablo inglés,
puedo ayudar a mi papá
y enseñar inglés a mis hermanitos.
Yo estoy orgulloso de mis dos idiomas,
pero a veces me siento como si
los que hablan español están en una montaña,
los que hablan inglés están en la otra,
y me gustaría empujarlos al río
para que todos estemos juntos.

CHAPTER 24:
MY JOURNEY TO EFFECTIVE MENTAL HEALTH THERAPY

"Voy a reir, voy a bailar, vivir mi vida, la la la la"
"I am going to laugh, I am going to dance, I'm going to live my life"
Marc Anthony- singer/songwriter

Access to effective mental health therapy changed the narrative of childhood abuse in my lifetime. In January 2020, at age 65, I finally found effective and meaningful mental health therapy with a therapist who understood my trauma from day one and has never minimized my school-based trauma as others had before her. I had tried mental health therapy several times since being diagnosed with PTSD in 1995 but nothing seemed to help or bring relief to my emotional pain. I continued to experience intrusive triggers at school throughout my professional career in *Colorado* and New Mexico.

I was referred to mental health therapy by a lawyer in December 2020 who witnessed my physical and emotional reaction in a child abuse deposition procedure where I was deposed. The legal claim involved a female student who reported the school based abuse of her principal. The defendant in this case was my former employer with a track record for sexually harassing his employees, but this was an elementary student! As his employee, I would be made to supervise the teacher from Mexico who reported him for sexual harassment and when I did not comply with his demand to fire her, I was terminated. I was hospitalized three days at the end of this school year with suicidal thoughts because I could not separate my own experiences in *Colorado* from the danger I felt working for this school official.

The fact that this victim was a child and he was a school official triggered my own childhood abuse in an unexpected way. The lawyer who had deposed me, would stop the procedures because I announced I wasn't feeling well. I was in a cold sweat at the moment and panicked by the circumstances. My red pullover sweater was soaking wet, my underclothes as well, my body was sweating excessively, my breathing erratic and I was shivering from the wet clothes now against my body. I didn't feel safe though I was in my home on a Zoom call with two lawyers and the defendant. I was shocked by my reaction but the lawyer was not, she recognized my PTSD symptoms and asked me if I had a therapist. I didn't at the time. She told me to wait for a phone call from a therapist within the hour.

True to her word, I got the phone call that launched me into effective mental health therapy for the first time in my life. I started therapy with Lana in the middle of the Covid outbreak using facetime and online platforms to meet on a bi-weekly basis.

The Miracle of EMDR

In one of our initial meetings, she would ask me if I knew the onset and source of my trauma and I responded in anger, "Lana, I've been fucked up for a long time." I then proceeded to tell her about the book I published seven months after retiring in 2017 from public education in New Mexico. I felt it was a valuable document at the time on many levels because it provided a history of my school-based trauma. I told her the book titled: <u>Shameful Violations: My Free and Public Education,</u> was no longer available online because I took it off the market one year after it was published. The "Me too Movement" which rose during the presidential campaign in 2016 triggered the years of silence I had learned to live with after reporting sexual harassment as an elementary principal in Colorado in 1995.

I related and identified with the experiences shared by the women of the "Me Too Movement" therefore I was being triggered to that unresolved conflict in my life. When I retired from public school teaching in New Mexico in December 2017 , I was having a PTSD relapse as I came to know the experience. A total recall of all school trauma, as a child and an adult female. In my book I referred to total recall as "the day the veils came down in my memory" and I would unravel emotionally.

In 2017, I was so broken, I could only write about myself in third person. My writing then was raw, angry and hard for me to read though

I had authored the story. It was an incomplete story however it did document my trauma from age six. I presented the trauma as *"Descansos"* /Resting places, times in my life when part of my character died or was under attack. The book sold poorly and I had no marketing plan. However, it achieved the goal of breaking 20 years of silence. I wrote of the long term effects of school based trauma from elementary school to my professional career in public schools. The missing link in my writing then was a lack of effective mental health therapy.

During the first month of therapy, I read my book <u>Shameful Violations</u> out loud to my therapist, I cried and expressed every emotion all the while. Reading my book out loud to her was therapeutic for me because writing the book had also become something else to be ashamed of in my life. Now it had purpose, it provided a documented timeline of the systemic racism from age six to the end of my school career and its long term effects in my career.

Lana educated me about EMDR, Eye Movement, Desensitization, and Reprocessing, a therapeutic approach for PTSD sufferers which she was versed in as a mental health therapist. She told me I would need more than "talking about" what happened, I had to confront, contend and resolve the trauma from the source in order to heal. I would purchase a Theratapper which provided tactile stimulation during therapy, basically a small control box where I set the controls for the session and attached are two small hand held tappers The tactile stimulation mirrored the anxiety felt during trauma when set to short fast intervals. I then hold the tappers in each hand as I focus on the work for today's session. My therapist explained that the bilateral stimulation between the tappers and my senses would effectively address the symptoms of PTSD.

At the beginning of each session, Lana will ask me the focus for today, where I felt the tension in my body and my beliefs about myself at that moment at that age. This was very hard to do in the beginning because I could not separate the present from the past memories. I had a hard time going back to first grade in 1962, that was a lifetime ago! It took practice to quiet my adult educated self in order to listen to the child's voice inside me. I began to make progress with my therapy once

I learned how to access my inner child and listen as she told me and showed me what happened in that classroom. I learned that the events of 1962 were the source of my trauma and therefore all other school events which occurred thereafter would lead back to that school year.

Desensitization: The D in EMDR

With each session, I began to desensitize the emotions and feelings associated with my teacher at age six. Before this breakthrough in my therapy, I could only see myself as an educated female whose views were blurred by anger, shame, depression, hostility and anxiety. I was afraid of meeting my child self and so I had to overcome that fear in order to move forward. The therapist coached me to understand what my child self needed from my adult self, was a lot of love, acceptance and to assure she was safe now and forever. I was then able to be in the classroom with my childhood self and observe the teachers' behaviors in class and at her apartment. This was powerful for me to accomplish because I felt like my own advocate watching and recording the daily events at school. This breakthrough in my therapy helped me recover memories which filled the gaps of my memory.

As I desensitized from the childhood trauma, it became more natural and satisfying to express love to self and to assure my safety in all aspects of my life. I began to see myself worthy of God's love as never before. I became more aware of the toxins I had poured into my body to mask the pain of delayed trauma and began to break free of bad habits. I began to reclaim relationships with significant people which I had not allowed myself to access for years. The overwhelming fear of their judgment and criticism had limited my relationships with members of my own family and school colleagues.

This simple device empowered me to control the anxiety in my body by turning down the tactile stimulation to longer and slower intervals, my breathing now calm and controlled. This was a huge accomplishment for someone who had lived with severe anxiety for years! I would experience severe anxiety driving to a professional meeting by myself, taking my granddaughter to lunch or driving to a doctor's office. I had no confidence in my driving skills or being able to find the place I needed to be. I would experience anxiety walking down a hallway full of students and adults. I would experience overwhelming anxiety taking a test to administer standardized English tests at school.

My Safe Place

The last stage of my weekly therapy session is dedicated to "the container", a mental dump to dispose of the painful memories and events which surfaced that day and during the week. I imagine myself standing over an open port where all negative thoughts and memories are flushed out with a constant flow of warm water from head to toe that gently replaces the water inside my body dirty from all the memories. . At this point in the therapy, my body is pain free and my mind is clear of thought. Now I go to my "safe place" in my mind where I feel safe. My safe spot is a spot along the *San Juan* river near my birthplace in *Colorado.* I used to play there when mom and I were working on the garden. I would be allowed to sit at the edge of the river where the water pooled enough for me to soak in its warmth mid morning. I caught tadpoles and watched them swim freely around me.

It is here where I rejoin my childhood self, *Elena,* my Spanish nickname used by my parents. This special name was *un carino-* an endearment from my parents who named each of their children in Spanish only to have catholic clergy rename us in English. Now as an adult in therapy my name *Elena* is symbolic with healing and reclaiming myself.

My adult and child self spend time holding each other, caressing each other's skin, being joyful and expressing love to each other. This when I know healing has occurred for both my adult and child personas, it's amazing! The reunion between my adult and child self has been joyous and so rewarding. I love the days *Elena* takes me for a walk along the river, past our garden and the wall of *"jaras*/willows" to a small sandy beach by the river. There, we would lay in the sand, stare at the sky and listen to the river. I love the days we swam together freely, floating on our backs and looking up at the clear blue sky above. We were swimming in the river without the fear of water I grew up with as a child. My journey toward reprocessing between past and present had begun. I was on my way to understanding what happened by having a conversation with my person at age six. I was in awe of the recovered memories which surfaced and filled in the missing pieces.

The Healing Light

The last step of weekly therapy is to bask in a soft yellow healing light which rains down on *Elena* and I as we hold each other. This healing light penetrates every inch of our body and has the capacity to repair damage from trauma, anger, anxiety and pain with a warm light. I am totally absorbed by this healing light, my body calm and receptive. I actually feel its warmth radiating throughout my body. I am completely relaxed and at peace with the work completed in this session. I leave therapy with a clear mind and closer to my goal. I hold Elena close as I hug myself in this moment of pure reclamation.

I have been under Lana's care since 2020 and use a Theratapper during therapy sessions. Lana is a gifted mental health therapist who is well read and knowledgeable on subjects like systemic racism, sexism, classism, homophobia and religious hate. We met twice weekly for the first year, it took time for me to learn the routine and therapeutic plan behind EMDR. I had to retrain my brain to accept a process of healing and improving my quality of life.

I owe so much of my healing to Lana's expertise and knowledge on the subject of school based trauma. She was part of a project of social workers who traveled to Native American reservations in the United States and Canada to investigate child abuse in Residential boarding schools. I knew then I was in good hands once she also told me her background of working in BIA schools in the southwest. She had heard the horror stories from tribal members who experienced and survived Residential Boarding school practices which left many crippled by the trauma imposed by Catholic clergy and public school educators. For the first time in my life I was being listened to by a professional therapist who could relate to my school trauma and its inhumanity. She has been the voice of healing for me since.

My journey has taught me that my professional career as a public-school teacher and elementary principal complicated and delayed access to effective mental health therapy for over (40) forty years of my life. While I was still an employee of any school district, I was prone to triggers which confused and disrupted my abilities to perform my duties whatever the title. I didn't dare to talk about what I was feeling at school, instead I would go look for a job in another district. I could never connect the dots between my behavior and the events at school.

Today, I have connected the dots between behavior and events at school. I know what happened to me at school and its effects in my life. I invested in effective mental health therapy for myself, because I knew it was not too late for me to heal from child abuse. I trust my therapist and her guidance; the results are the recovered memories which tell the story of what happened during the School Year 1962 and its effects on my professional career.

Reprocessing: The R in EMDR

As I began to reprocess the trauma, I returned to writing as an effective means to recover the memories and put them in order as they surfaced. It is in writing about the trauma I experienced as a child that I will achieve closure to this painful chapter in my life. I began writing in June of 2023, unsure of the outcome but determined to talk about what happened on paper. I knew that "talking about what happened" was vital to my recovery, yet I did not know where to find such a support group for my kind of trauma. I would have loved to be able to find others in life who had experienced the kind of trauma I had, but that did not happen for me. Perhaps my book will change that narrative for the many trapped in their painful school memories.

My therapy sessions were one to one and a half hours per week, which were focused sessions that began and ended within ninety minutes. As I began to write, I found myself being able to push past the trauma frame by frame without stopping because time was up. I found I could write for four hours or more and work through the darkness of trauma with confidence and I was talking on paper like never before!

At the end of each writing session, my body was aching and in pain! First, I sat for four hours, writing about the trauma that consumed my life for some time. Sitting and writing for that long time was unnatural to me and took a toll on my old body. I had pushed past some painful and shameful school events which were once impossible for me to even describe, let alone talk about the details and players involved. I was finally telling my "untold story" and letting go of my painful past in public schools.

I am not sad at the end of my writing sessions any longer! I am elated and happy about my process and the effectiveness of my therapy! I want to celebrate, but I still find myself alone in my jubilation.

The Silver linings of my life journey

Today, I enjoy several silver linings to my journey as I recover. The first silver lining to my life journey is I have never lost the passion for teaching and sharing knowledge with others. I still love organizing and planning instruction for my students of all ages! I have taught and administered first through sixth grades schools over a thirty five (35) year career in public education. As a retired bilingual teacher, I provide home school services for parents of students who are displaced in public education. I am also an Adult ESL instructor to Spanish speakers who value the fact I can understand and teach in two languages. I also teach Spanish to Adults who want to reclaim their Spanish voices or are ready to use their Spanish voices publicly.

The other silver lining is that I have reclaimed the six-year-old who was a gifted bilingual speaker at age six and became the teacher she needed. As a bilingual teacher, I continue to advocate for an educational system that is designed so students learn and speak more than one language in their lifetime without punishment or oppression. Afterall, two is more than one when it comes to linguistic intelligence.

The final silver lining is that I have forgiven myself for the years I doubted my career choice and could not understand my determination to continue in public education after the childhood trauma surfaced. In forgiving myself, I have forgiven those whose self hate I internalized while at school and carried as trauma in life.

I know I will never forget what happened at school for the rest of my life but in writing this book these experiences are documented and no longer my secret. They are a lesson for America.

"You cannot uneducate the person who has learned to read.
You cannot humiliate the person who feels pride.
You cannot oppress the people who are not afraid anymore."
Cesar Chavez- born March 31, 1927

Mi Despedida- My Farewell

Today, the words of this song are an anthem to my recovery and reclamation of self. I learned this elementary song from a gifted teacher in *Colorado* who loved to sing with our students and accompanied us with her beautiful piano playing. As a teacher, I would wait for that teachable moment when my students needed a pep talk about feeling good about themselves and needed to hear the words that described how special we are as human beings, then I would invite them to sing along with me. I never learned the author of this song, but am so thankful I never forgot the words.

I Feel Just Right in the Skin I Wear

I have feelings, and you do, too. I'd like to share a few with you,
Sometimes I'm happy, sometimes I'm sad, sometimes scared, and sometimes mad,
But the most important feeling you see, is that I am proud of being me!

(Chorus)
I feel just right in the skin I wear, there is no one like me anywhere,
I feel just right in the skin I wear, there is no one like me anywhere.

It's a wonderful thing, how everyone owns, just enough skin to cover his bones,
My dad's would be too big to fit, I'd be all wrinkled inside of it.
Baby sisters would be much too small, it wouldn't cover me up at all.
(Chorus)
I feel just right in the skin I wear, there is no one like me anywhere.
I feel just right in the skin I wear, there is no one like me anywhere.

No one sees the things I see, behind my eyes is only me.
And no one knows where my feelings begin, for there's only me inside my skin.
No one does what I can do, I'll be me and you be You.

(Chorus)
I feel just right in the skin I wear, there is no one like me anywhere.
I feel just right in the skin I wear, there is no one like me anywhere.

El Fin- The End

ABOUT THE AUTHOR

Gloria E. Lopez completed her BA-Bachelor of Arts degree at Adams State College in Alamosa, Colorado. In 1977, she earned a degree in Elementary Education with a double minor in Bilingual Education and Mexican American Studies.

In 1990, she earned her MA- Master of Arts degree from Colorado State University in Fort Collins Colorado with an area of study in Instructional Leadership.

She started her teaching career in Colorado in 1977. Ms. Lopez retired from public education in New Mexico in 2017.